Dear Reader,

Welcome to Southern Cross, a vast Australian cattle property in the Star Valley and home to Reid, Kane and Annie McKinnon.

There really is a beautiful and remote Star Valley, and it's situated to the north of Townsville, where I live. The Broken and Star Rivers flow through this district, and the cattle stations there have wonderful names like Starlight, Starbright and ZigZag. However, there are no towns in the valley, and although I have made Southern Cross station and the township of Mirrabrook as authentic as I can, they are entirely my creations.

I am thrilled to be bringing you three linked stories about the McKinnon family's secrets. In this book, Annie leaves the Outback—for the bright city lights of Brisbane—to meet a man she's met in an Internet chat group. Will she find her perfect man in the city?

Happy reading, and my warmest wishes,

Barbara Hannay

THE BLIND DATE SURPRISE

Barbara Hannay

Southern Cross Ranch

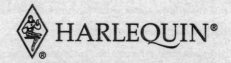
HARLEQUIN®

TORONTO • NEW YORK • LONDON
AMSTERDAM • PARIS • SYDNEY • HAMBURG
STOCKHOLM • ATHENS • TOKYO • MILAN • MADRID
PRAGUE • WARSAW • BUDAPEST • AUCKLAND

Special thanks to Andrea and Gordon Smith,
my eyes and ears in Brisbane.

ISBN 0-373-18191-4

THE BLIND DATE SURPRISE

First North American Publication 2005.

PROLOGUE

FROM the Ask Auntie page of the *Mirrabrook Star*. (Circulation 2,500, including Wallaby Flats):

> *Ask Auntie,*
> *The loneliness of the outback is driving me crazy. I'm two hundred kilometres from the nearest cinema or nightclub and it's so hard to meet guys. The few dates I've had have been spectacularly forgettable, but now I've met a wonderfully warm, funny and clever man over the Internet and I'm in love. I want to dash off to the city to meet him, but all my life I've been accused of being too hasty and impulsive, so I'm seeking guidance. What do you advise?*
> *Marooned in Mirrabrook.*

> *Dear Marooned in Mirrabrook,*
> *If you're as lonely as you sound and your cyber-romance is going well, why shouldn't*

you meet this man? I suspect you're afraid of disappointment—that you fear you've fallen in love with the idea of the man, but you're worried about the reality. Some tension is understandable, but if you're looking for a long-term relationship you need real interaction with a real man. You need to meet him.

Of course, a woman from the bush would be wise to approach an e-date in the city with some caution. Perhaps you could arrange for a double date with friends? If not, you should make sure you meet at a public venue and you should have a friend in the city who knows the time and location of your date and who can be reached at the touch of a button on your mobile phone.

However, once these details are organised, go for it. Don't believe the old cliché that good things come to those who wait. Good things come to people who want them so badly they can't sit still...

Good luck!

Ask Auntie.

CHAPTER ONE

CRIKEY, *pink* jeans!

Annie McKinnon hated to guess what her brothers would say if they could see her. Come to think of it, what would anyone from her outback home town, Mirrabrook, say? She'd lived in blue denim jeans since she was three years old—ever since her brother, Kane, first lifted her on to the back of a stock horse.

Never pink. And *never* teamed with stilettos.

And yet here she was in the heart of the city, sashaying into the foyer of one of Brisbane's swankiest hotels in killer heels, the sweetest little white silk camisole top, and low-rise jeans so baby-pink and slim she felt like a pop-star wannabe.

So this was where following your friends' advice got you.

'You'd better listen to Victoria,' Melissa had said. 'She's our in-house fashionista and everyone at work takes her word as gospel.'

Victoria had been definite. 'Annie, when it's

an e-date, you have to be super careful. You need to hit exactly the right note.'

And because Annie had known Melissa since boarding school, and because Victoria was Mel's flatmate, and because both the girls were city born and bred, Annie had deferred to their finely honed understanding of 'How Things Work in the City'.

The trio had hit the shops with Victoria leading the fray, and Annie had quickly discovered how exceedingly lucky she was to have clued-up friends to advise her about clothes. On her own, she would have made so *totally* all the wrong choices.

She'd wanted to head straight for the stunning racks of sparkly after-five wear, but Victoria had dismissed them with a disdainful toss of the corkscrew curls she'd created that morning.

'No way, Annie. You don't want to look as if you're trying too hard to impress Damien. If you look too dressed up or trendy you might scare him off.'

Oh.

After one last wistful glance towards the shimmering, ultra-feminine dresses, Annie allowed herself to be steered towards racks of jeans.

'Never underestimate jeans,' Victoria explained with impressive patience. 'You can dress them up or down and they always look fab.'

'But—um—I live in jeans. And Damien knows I'm a country girl. Don't you think these might make me look a little too *Annie Get Your Gun*?'

Victoria blinked, then eyed Annie with just a tad more respect. 'Point taken.'

But, seconds later, she was struck by her light bulb idea. 'I've got it! *Pink* jeans would be perfect. Team them with a little camisole top.' Grabbing a coat-hanger from a rack, she flourished something white and silky. *'How heaven is this?'*

Annie squashed the thought that a pink and white outfit would make her look like an ice cream. She tried the clothes on and decided that they were comfortable *and* rather gorgeous, actually.

But she put up a stronger fight over the high heels.

'What if Damien's really short?'

This time Mel chipped in. 'He didn't look short in the photo he sent you.'

'Photos can be deceptive.' Annie had spent many sleepless nights worrying about that possibility.

'Annie, if Damien's short, you're going to

be taller than him no matter what kind of shoes
you wear.'

She tried another tack. 'I can't afford two
hundred and fifty dollars for a couple of strips
of sequinned leather.'

Victoria grinned. 'Don't worry, that's why
God invented credit cards.'

And so here she was in the foyer of the
Pinnacle Hotel, dressed by Victoria and getting
last-minute advice from both the girls before
she took the lift to La Piastra on the twenty-
seventh floor. To meet Damien.

Damien. *Eeeeeee!* Just thinking about him
made her stomach play leap-frog with her
heart. She knew it was foolish to have high
hopes for this guy, but she couldn't help it.
She'd travelled over a thousand kilometres
from her outback cattle station in Southern
Cross, North Queensland, just to meet him and
she really, *really* wanted their date to work out.

It was going to be fine. It *was*.

Everything she and Damien had chatted
about over the Internet during the past six
weeks indicated that they meshed. They both
loved dogs, world music, books and thinking
about deeper things—like destiny and fate,
whether life was a wager, and the possibility
that animals were happier than humans.
Talking to him had been comfortable and in-

spiring, fun and—and well, to be honest—
sexy.

To cap it off, she and Damien both adored
everything Italian, *especially* linguini.

That was why they'd settled on La Piastra.

And when Damien had emailed her a photo
of himself, she'd completely flipped. Head
over heels. He looked so-o-o yummy—with
sleepy blue eyes, sun-streaked surfer-boy hair,
pash-me-now lips and a cute, crooked smile.
She hoped to high heaven that he'd been as
impressed with *her* photo as he'd claimed to
be, because she could feel in her bones that he
was her perfect match.

And now she was about to meet him.

She was six minutes late, which, according
to Mel and Victoria, was perfect timing. Her
heart thumped as the trio waited for the lift,
and she drew several deep breaths while the
girls pumped her with last-minute advice.

'Remember, don't be too serious. Try to relax and have fun.'

'But don't drink too much.'

'You have to watch your date's body language. If he's mirroring your gestures, you're
on the right track.'

'The danger sign is when he crosses his
arms while you're talking.'

'Or if he starts to come on too heavy. He might just want sex.'

Annie shook her head to shush them. The girls meant well, but she wasn't as clueless about men as they feared. Besides, there was a rather conservative, bespectacled fellow a few feet behind Victoria, who must have overheard them. He was looking rather stunned by their conversation and he—*crikey*—he almost walked smack into a marble pillar.

Annie was about to send him a sympathetic smile when the bell above the lift pinged.

The doors were about to open.

'Remember there's always the escape plan,' Mel urged. 'You've got your mobile phone handy, haven't you?'

'Yes.'

'Right. You look gorgeous, Annie.'

'Stunning!'

'Thanks.'

'So break a leg!'

'Have a ball!'

'Go get Damien, kiddo!'

Amidst a flurry of air kisses Annie stepped into the lift, sent the girls a quick wave, and pressed the button for Level twenty-seven. The doors swished closed, Mel and Victoria's encouraging grins disappeared, and with a soft sigh the lift whisked her away from them... skywards.

And her stomach dropped. Oh, crumbs.

She made a last-minute check in the mirror at the back of the lift. No bra showing, no visible panty-line. Lipstick still holding. Hair okay.

Ping! Level twenty-seven.

Gulp.

This was it.

The lift doors swept apart and Annie looked out at an expanse of mega-trendy pale timber and stainless steel. So this was La Piastra. She felt a fleeting rush of nostalgia for Beryl's friendly café in Mirrabrook with its gingham tablecloths, ruffled curtains and bright plastic flowers on every table.

How silly. She'd come to Brisbane to get away from all that. Somewhere in here Damien was waiting. *Oh, please let him like me.* Her legs shook. She was as nervous as she'd been on her first day at boarding school.

A tall, dark, very Italian-looking man in black was watching her from his post directly in front of the lift and as she approached him he bowed stiffly.

'Good evening, madam.'

'Good evening.'

'Welcome to La Piastra.' He looked down a very Roman nose at her.

'Thanks.' She smiled, but her smile faltered as the man waited for her to say something more. What was she supposed to say? She peered into the restaurant, searching for a streaked sandy head among the diners. 'I'm—er—supposed to be meeting someone here.'

'You have a reservation?'

'No.'

He frowned and pursed his lips.

She hurried to explain. 'I mean *I* don't actually have a reservation, but I've come to meet someone—who made a reservation.'

Cringe! Was she a country hick making a complete fool of herself, or what?

He turned to a thick book on a timber and stainless steel lectern. 'What name?'

'You mean his name?'

Her question was met by a sigh that suggested the man in black was quite certain he was dealing with an airhead. 'What name was given when the reservation was made?'

'Grainger,' she said with sudden dignity. 'Mr Damien Grainger.'

Again he peered down his imperious Roman nose and slowly examined the list of names in his book. And Annie felt a moment's panic. Could she have made a mistake? Was this the wrong restaurant…the wrong day, wrong time?

No, it couldn't be. She'd checked and re-checked Damien's email a thousand times.

She peered again into the restaurant. She'd been hoping that Damien would keep an eye out for her. She'd pictured him leaping to his feet when he saw her, hurrying through the restaurant to meet her, his face alight with a welcoming smile.

Perhaps his table was positioned behind a post?

'Ah, yes,' said the rich Italian voice at her side. 'Table thirty-two.'

Phew.

'But I'm afraid Mr Grainger hasn't arrived yet.'

Oh.

Silly of her, but she'd been certain that Damien would be on time, even early.

'Would you care to wait for him at the bar or at your table?'

She glanced at the bar. If she waited there, perched on a stool by herself, she would feel like a prize lemon. 'At the table, please.'

'Then come this way.'

Several heads turned as she followed him to a table set for two near a window. Back in Mirrabrook, people would have been smiling and calling out greetings. Here they merely stared without emotion. Was there something wrong with the way she looked? Were her jeans too pink?

A seat was drawn out for her.

Annie sat and looked at the bare, pale timber table top, set with two round black linen place mats and starched white napkins, solid shining cutlery, gleaming wineglasses and a single square black candle exactly in the middle of a square white saucer.

It was all very urban. Very minimalist.

If Damien had been here, she would have found it exciting.

'Would you care for a drink while you're waiting?'

She tried to remember the name of the trendy drink Mel had ordered for her at a bar the night before. Something with cranberry juice.

When she hesitated, the man in black asked, 'Perhaps you would like to see our wine list?'

'No, thank you. Um, would it be all right if I just have water for now?'

'Certainly. Would you prefer still or sparkling?'

Good grief. At Beryl's café in Mirrabrook, water was simple, uncomplicated H_2O.

'Still water, please.'

He left her then and Annie heaved a sigh of relief. But the relief was only momentary, because now she was very conscious of being alone. A swift glance around her showed that she was the only person in the restaurant sitting by herself.

Shoulders back, Annie. You can't let a little thing like that throw you.

A handsome young waiter approached her, bearing a tray with a frosted bottle of iced water. 'How are you this evening?' he asked, smiling.

She smiled back and the simple act of sharing a smile made her feel a little better. 'Very well, thank you.'

'I'm Roberto and I'll be looking after your table.'

Her smile held. 'I'm Annie and I'll be looking forward to your service.'

His mouth stretched into a broad grin as he poured water into her glass. 'Would you like to see our menu?'

'No, I'll wait for my—' She indicated the empty seat opposite her.

'Girlfriend?'

'Actually, no—it's a guy.'

He managed to look charmingly disappointed before moving away to take orders from a nearby table.

Annie took a sip of water and wished she could press the cool glass against her hot cheeks. She told herself that it didn't matter that Damien was late. He was probably battling his way though a traffic jam, cursing fate. Any minute now he'd come bursting out of the lift, full of apologies.

She counted to a hundred and then took another sip. After reaching three hundred and taking more sips, she watched a couple on the other side of the room reach across their table to hold hands then gaze romantically into each other's eyes.

Somewhere in the background a guitar was playing *Beautiful Dreamer*.

Sigh. How many hours had she spent dreaming about this date in the city? About what Damien would think of her, what she'd think of him.

She'd worried about saying the wrong things, or discovering that he had some terrible off-putting habit. She'd considered endless ways to suss out whether he was married. That was her biggest fear. But she'd never once imagined that she would be sitting here alone. Without him.

The worst thing was that on her own in the city, surrounded by people, she felt even lonelier than she did in the outback, when she was surrounded by nothing but gumtrees and wild mountains.

She turned to look out of the window at the lights in the tall buildings around her, at the flickering neon signs in the distance, at the street lights way below and the headlights and tail-lights of the traffic—red and white rivers flowing in opposite directions...

Where was Damien?

Perhaps she should have given him her mobile phone number, but she'd been playing it cautious until she met him. Now she was tempted to ring Mel and Victoria just for a little friendly reassurance, but she resisted the urge.

She didn't want to look at her watch. Oh, well, perhaps a quick glimpse. Oh, God. Damien was twenty-five minutes late.

Maybe this was a guy thing. Damien was establishing the upper hand, making her wait. And wait...

Around her, people's meals were arriving. The food was served on enormous white plates. Someone was having linguini drizzled with a pale green sauce and it looked divine.

Roberto came back and asked her if there was anything else he could bring her. Some bruschetta, perhaps? She shook her head, but she realised that other diners were casting curious glances her way. Again.

Oh, Damien. I know you probably can't help it, but this is so disappointing.

How much longer would she have to wait?

When the waiter left, Annie fingered her cute new clutch handbag and reconsidered using her phone to have a quick chat with the girls. But as she flicked the clasp she saw the man who guarded the front of the restaurant walking towards her. What now? Was he going to ask her to order some food or leave?

'Miss McKinnon?' he said as he approached.

'Yes?' Her stomach lurched. How did he know her name?

'We've received a phone call—a message from Mr Grainger.'

'Yes?' she said again and her heart jolted painfully.

'He's had to cancel this evening's engagement.'

Cancel?

Whoosh! Slam! Annie felt as if she'd been tipped through the window and was falling to the pavement twenty-seven floors below.

Damien couldn't cancel. Not like this. 'No,' she squeaked. 'That's not possible. There must be a mistake.'

The man in black's jaw clenched.

Wrong thing to say.

She tried again. 'Did—did Mr Grainger say why he has cancelled?'

She must have looked totally stricken because his face softened a fraction. 'I'm afraid the person who rang didn't offer an explanation. He asked me to apologise, Miss McKinnon. Apparently he's been trying to ring for some time, but our line has been busy. He hopes you will understand.'

Understand? Of course she didn't understand. She couldn't possibly understand. Annie felt so suddenly awful she wondered if she was going to be sick right there in front of everyone. 'Didn't he tell you *anything*? Are you sure he didn't—explain—?'

The man sighed and shook his head as if he found this situation tiresome.

'What should I do?' she asked. 'Do—do I owe you any money?'

'No. And you are still very welcome to dine here. The caller is happy to pay for your meal.'

The caller? Nothing made sense. 'Damien Grainger called, didn't he?'

'No, it was Mr Grainger's uncle.'

His *uncle*? This was really crazy. Where was Damien? Why hadn't he rung? Was he sick? Oh, goodness, yes. That had to be the problem. Damien was suddenly, horribly, unavoidably, violently ill. From his sickbed he'd begged this uncle to phone her.

'Shall I send for a menu?' the man asked her.

Annie shook her head. Her throat was so choked she couldn't speak and there was no way she could possibly think about eating. Not in the midst of tragedy. This was the single worst moment in her life.

Grabbing her bag, she managed to stand and then she took a deep breath and began to walk...past the other tables...conscious of the unbearable curiosity of the diners. Holding her head high and her shoulders back, she stared straight ahead, not wanting to catch anyone's eye.

It wasn't until she was safely out of the restaurant and behind the closed doors of the lift that she collapsed against the wall and covered her mouth with her hand and tried to hold back the horrible sobs that swelled in her throat and burned her. Was it possible to bear this disappointment, this horrible humiliation?

As the lift cruised downwards, she fumbled in her purse for her phone.

'Mel,' she sobbed as soon as there was an answer.

'Annie, where are you?'

'I'm in the lift at the Pinnacle.'

'Why? Are you running away?'

'Yes.'

'Oh, my God, what happened?'

'*Nothing!* Where are you?'

'Just up the road,' Mel shouted above a blast of loud background music. 'At The Cactus Flower. It's in the next block from where you are—on the left.'

'Stay there, please. I'm coming.'

'Honey, we won't move.'

Theo Grainger waited in the foyer of the Pinnacle Hotel and watched the blinking lights in the panel beside the lift indicating its journey downward from the twenty-seventh floor. All too soon, those shiny lift doors would slide open and Annie McKinnon would burst out.

A kind of dread tightened his throat muscles as he anticipated the tears streaming down her face. The kid would be a mess. A heartbroken, disillusioned mess.

He cursed himself for handling the whole situation so badly. His cowardly, fickle nephew had caused enough trouble, but Theo had bungled his part in the evening too.

He wasn't sure how he'd managed to make such a hash of things. He'd come to the hotel this evening with the best of intentions. He'd planned to meet the young Internet hopeful and to apologise to her on his nephew's behalf and to explain that the date had been cancelled. To apologise in person—before she headed up to La Piastra.

Theo could pile on the charm when necessary and he'd been confident he could appease Damien's date and send her on her way with her dignity intact, even if her tender young heart was broken. It wasn't the first time he'd had to move into damage control after one of his nephew's pranks.

But somehow Theo hadn't been prepared for Annie McKinnon.

He hadn't anticipated the blinding excitement shining in her face. She'd arrived at the Pinnacle looking so incredibly young and innocent, so unspeakably hopeful. So thrilled!

And he *certainly* hadn't anticipated her cheer squad of friends.

The girlfriends had been his final stumbling block. One mere male couldn't be expected to confront *three* overexcited, chattering females with the bad news that the *big deal* date was off.

In future, he would make sure that Damien was forced to face up to the consequences of his thoughtless pranks, even if he had to drag the wretch to the scene of his crime by the scruff of his neck.

But tonight the result of Theo's bungling was that he'd felt a compunction to hang around for the aftermath—to make sure Annie McKinnon wasn't too terribly heartbroken.

The light beside the lift indicated that it had reached the ground floor and he stood to one side of the foyer with his hands plunged deep in his trouser pockets. There was a clean handkerchief in his right pocket and it would come in handy if he needed to mop her tears before he called a taxi to send her safely homewards.

The doors opened and he held his breath and steeled himself for the sight of Annie's flushed, tear-ravaged face.

But no.

Annie swept out of the lift with her golden head high, looking pale but dignified, almost haughty. No sign of tears. Her pretty blue eyes were dry and glass-clear and her mouth was composed, almost smiling.

Almost. If Theo hadn't been watching her very closely, he might have missed the tremor of her chin and the exceedingly careful way she walked, as if she needed all her strength to hold herself together.

Her unexpected courage shook him. He felt

a sudden lump in his throat and an absurd urge to applaud her.

And he remained stock-still as she sailed across the foyer. Even as the huge glass doors at the hotel's entrance parted, he didn't move. It made absolutely no sense but this devastated young woman seemed more composed than he felt.

She disappeared into the night before he came to his senses. By the time he dashed outside she was already hurrying along the footpath, ducking her way past pedestrians with athletic grace.

He called, 'Annie!'

But she didn't hear him and when people turned and stared at him he felt several versions of foolish. What on earth had he thought he was going to do if she'd heard him? Offer her coffee and consolation?

Clearly she needed neither.

He came to a halt in the middle of the footpath. Ahead of him, he saw a flash of pink jeans and white top as Annie turned to her left. Then she hurried up a short flight of steps and vanished inside a bar.

Theo Grainger couldn't remember the last time he'd felt so inadequate.

*   *   *

'The guy's a jerk!'

'An A-grade jerk.'

Mel and Victoria were vehement in their anger.

And never had Annie been happier to see friends.

As the three girls drowned their sorrows in strawberry daiquiris, she found it comforting to listen to their united rant.

'Annie, your Damien has reached an entirely new, utterly despicable level of jerkdom.'

'How dare he behave so jerkily to such a lovely, trusting country mouse?'

But the horrible part was that in between moments of righteous anger Annie still wanted to love Damien. She couldn't let go of her fantasy man in the blink of an eye. She needed to believe he was helpless and guiltless.

Perhaps he really couldn't have helped missing the date. There was still a chance that he was sick, in pain and feeling as bitterly disappointed as she was.

'He might be sick,' she said wistfully.

Victoria sniffed. 'Yeah, that's about as likely as he's fallen under a bus.'

'Or he's found an urgent need to flee the country,' added Mel, rolling her eyes. 'Face it, Annie. If Damien was halfway decent and he had a genuine excuse, he would have gone out of his way to make sure you understood what had kept him.'

Annie sighed. 'I suppose you're right... I guess I just don't want to believe it.'

It was so hard to let go of her happy dreams. She wanted to crawl away and cry for a month.

'The thing is,' said Mel, stirring her icy daiquiri with a slim black straw. 'He's not just a base-level jerk, he's a cowardly jerk. He had to pretend to be someone else.'

'What do you mean?'

'I bet you any cocktail on this menu that the so-called uncle who relayed the message doesn't exist.'

The thought that it might have actually been Damien on the phone, pretending to be someone else, made Annie feel ten times worse.

Victoria patted her shoulder. 'I reckon you should forget about blind dates and concentrate on raising the cocktail drinking statistics for the Greater Brisbane Area.'

Annie nodded miserably. It wasn't her style, but losing herself in an alcoholic fuzz had definite appeal. The problem was that it would only take the edge off her pain momentarily. There would still be tomorrow. And the rest of the week in Brisbane. A whole week in the city. Without Damien.

'I'd rather go back to your place and borrow your computer to send The Jerk a blistering email,' she said.

'Yeah,' agreed Mel. 'Great idea. Besides, Victoria and I still have to go to work tomorrow morning. Let's go home and send Damien a message he won't forget. Let's make sure he absolutely understands just how totally bottom-of-the-pits he's been.'

'If he's a true jerk, it'll be like water off a duck's back,' suggested Victoria gloomily.

But Mel's mind was made up. 'It doesn't matter. Annie will feel a lot better once we've told him off.'

CHAPTER TWO

Tossing and turning on the lumpy old couch in Mel's lounge, Annie stared into the darkness. This was the worst night of her life. She was never going to sleep.

After helping her compose the email designed to set Damien back on his heels, Mel and Victoria had gone off to their bedrooms and were sound asleep now. Annie was left to get through the long night alone. And, to her dismay, the satisfaction she'd felt when she'd hit the button to shoot their message into cyber space was evaporating.

Rolling on to her side, she punched her pillow and gave vent to a loud groan. It echoed through the house, but no one stirred. That was the one good thing about loneliness; she didn't have to be brave any more. She could finally wallow in her misery.

Now, in a cocoon of silence and darkness, she could tell herself that never in the history of dating had there been a bigger fiasco, and if there had been she didn't want to know about it. Her experience at La Piastra was as bad as it got.

She could admit to herself that she was truly devastated. Devastated, hurt to the marrow, disappointed to the max! And angry. Yeah, bitter too.

Her *glorious romance* was over before it had begun.

How could Damien have done this to her?

How could he have spent so many weeks courting her in writing, just to leave her stranded at the Big Moment?

And *why*? What had gone wrong? Had she been too forward when she'd suggested they should meet? Should she have waited till he'd broached the subject? The thing was, he'd shown no sign of caution or of having cold feet. Once she'd mentioned the idea of a date he had seemed very keen.

His absence didn't make sense and she couldn't let go of the slim hope that something completely unavoidable had detained him. Problem was, if that was the case, he wouldn't appreciate the savage email the girls had encouraged her to send.

Oh, hell!

It seemed like agonising hours later that she banged the pillow with another thump and flung herself on to her back, still too tense to sleep. Mel's house was in the inner city, not far from a main road, and as she listened to the alien sounds of never-ending traffic, tears seeped beneath her stinging eyelids and she felt a rush of homesickness.

At home the day started when the sun peeped over the Seaview Range and she was nudged awake by her Border collie, Lavender. She would give anything to hear the reassuring thump of Lavender's tail on her bedroom floor. And at Southern Cross she'd be greeted by the friendly laughter of kookaburras and the warbling of magpies, or perhaps the distant soft lowing of cattle.

But thinking about home and her twin brothers, Reid and Kane, brought an added twinge of guilt. The guys had been away mustering cattle when she'd left for her adventure in the city. She'd left them a note, but because she'd been afraid they'd jump right in and put a stop to her plans, she hadn't told them any details.

In her own mind she'd justified her dash to the city. Apart from the compulsion to meet her e-date, she'd felt a strong need for a holiday. But she knew that people usually planned their holidays. They didn't dash away, leaving a note telling family members to look after themselves.

Perhaps she shouldn't have been so secretive. Surely she should have been able to tell at least one of her brothers about the man she'd met over the Internet. But they were so protective of her. Which was why she'd resorted to writing a letter to the *Mirrabrook Star*.

If only her mother wasn't so far away in Scotland...

But thinking about her family only made her feel lonelier than ever. As she waited for morning and for Damien's reply to her email, she almost reached the point where she wished that her brothers *had* stopped her from coming to the city.

'You got a reply.'

At breakfast, Mel came into the kitchen waving a sheet of A4 paper at Annie. 'Here, I printed it out.'

Pain jabbed hard in Annie's chest. There was no escaping the truth now. Very soon she would know Damien's reason for avoiding her.

'It's from the uncle,' Mel said as Annie snatched up the page.

'The *uncle*?' Annie clasped the paper to her chest, too disappointed to read it. 'It's not from Damien?'

''Fraid not.'

Victoria turned from the microwave where she was heating coffee. 'So there really is an uncle?'

'Looks like it,' said Mel, reaching for milk to pour on her cereal.

Annie groaned. 'You mean an *uncle* read that email we sent last night?'

'Seems so.'

'But we were so—' Annie gulped. 'So—'

'Tipsy,' supplied Mel, looking sheepish.

'And rude,' added Annie. 'I had no idea his uncle would read it. Heck, we should have toned it down.'

'Hey, don't sweat,' said Victoria. 'We were relatively sober and we were merely being honest. We told it like it was.'

'Yeah...but to some old uncle!' Annie cringed at the thought of a sweet, elderly uncle reading their message. It had sounded so forceful and feminist last night. But when she thought about it now...

Oh, crumbs...

Fearing the worst, she looked down at the page...

From: T. G. Grainger
To: anniem@mymail.com
Date: Monday, November 14th 6:05 a.m.
Subject: Re: You'd better have a brilliant excuse, you jerk!

Dear Annie M,
I hope you don't mind my replying to your message, but my nephew is out of town this

week and he's asked me to respond to any important emails. I consider your communication to be of the utmost importance. I regret having to intrude into such a personal exchange but I believe you deserve the courtesy of a quick response.

Please accept my sincerest apology for the unpleasant experience you suffered last night as a consequence of my nephew's inexcusable thoughtlessness.

Damien was called away at short notice and I contacted La Piastra restaurant on his behalf. However, I understand your deep distress and I am saddened by my nephew's bad manners. You're absolutely right; you deserved an explanation from him and I will make sure that he contacts you immediately on his return.

In the meantime, I trust that you are still able to enjoy the remainder of your stay in Brisbane.

Yours sincerely,
Dr Theo Grainger.

Annie dropped the page on to the tabletop. 'Oh, my God. Damien was called away at short notice.'

'Oh, yeah,' scoffed Mel. 'And we all came down in the last shower.'

'You don't believe him?'

This question was greeted by a significant silence while Annie watched Mel and Victoria exchange knowing glances that snuffed out her final glimmer of hope. After a bit, Victoria leaned across the table, grabbed the page and scanned the printed message.

'The uncle's a bit of a wordsmith, isn't he?'

Annie nodded sadly. 'I guess ''inexcusable thoughtlessness'' is a refined way of saying that his nephew's a bottom-of-the-pit jerk.'

Mel grinned. 'I rather liked the way we described his rotten nephew in *our* email.'

'Yeah,' said Victoria. 'There's nothing wrong with short, shoot-from-the-hip language.'

Annie managed a small smile.

'Anyway.' Victoria tapped a French tipped fingernail against the email printout. 'This uncle's a doctor, so you'd expect fancy words.'

'He's not a medical doctor,' said Mel.

Annie and Victoria stared at her. 'How do you know?' they both asked simultaneously.

'Because a Dr Theo Grainger was my philosophy lecturer at university and it's not a common name. I'm sure this must be the same guy.'

Annie's mouth fell open. 'You studied philosophy?'

'In my first year. I didn't keep it up because I wanted to major in urban planning, but Dr Grainger was a pretty cool lecturer. He had quite a following.'

To Annie the very word philosophy sounded lofty and unbelievably clever, and she found it hard to imagine an ordinary girlfriend like Mel studying the subject.

Suddenly Victoria looked at the clock. 'Hey, look at the time. We'd better get moving or we'll be late for work, Mel.'

The two girls jumped to their feet.

'Don't worry about the kitchen. I'll tidy up,' Annie called after them, but they'd already disappeared into their rooms. It occurred to her that if she stayed in their house much longer the girls would soon treat her the way her brothers did.

At home, Kane and Reid ran around doing important outside work like mustering the cattle, fencing, servicing the bores and machinery, and they left her behind to cook and clean and keep the books, as if she were some outback version of Cinderella.

It was a big part of the reason she'd wanted to get away and it wasn't very comforting to think that in no time at all she was becoming a City Girl Cinders.

A broken-hearted, disillusioned City Girl Cinders.

One thing was sure; she didn't want to spend this week keeping Mel and Victoria's flat clean and tidy. But what were her options? She could reply to Dr Grainger's email and press the issue about Damien by demanding to know when he'd be back. But she was fast losing confidence in the Internet as a form of honest communication.

She lifted the printout from the table and read the uncle's email again. Philosophers were fantastically brilliant and thoughtful and wise, weren't they? Pity some of it hadn't rubbed off on his nephew.

Actually, it was a wonder this philosopher uncle hadn't lectured *her* on her own lack of wisdom. No doubt he took a rather dim view of any girl who dashed recklessly into the city from the far reaches of the outback and expected a blind date to fulfil her silly romantic fantasies.

She was halfway across the kitchen with cereal packets in hand when she paused. Come to think of it, Uncle Theo hadn't expressed any negative opinions about her. He'd been surprisingly sympathetic.

Perhaps there was something deeper behind

this—something the uncle understood. A direct approach to Dr Grainger might sort this whole mess out. Rather than mucking around with email, it would be better to deal with him face-to-face. That was the McKinnon way. It was what her brothers would do.

Look the enemy in the eye so you knew what you were dealing with.

But how the heck did you confront a philosopher?

'Dropping the dishcloth, she dashed into the bathroom, where Mel was applying mascara.

'Which university does this Dr Grainger teach at?'

Mel frowned at her reflection in the mirror. 'UQ at St Lucia. Why?'

'I—I've always been curious about philosophy and I was thinking that, as I have time on my hands, it might be interesting to sneak into the back of one of his lectures. Is that allowed?'

'Well…yes.' Mel gave her eyelashes a final flick with the mascara wand and turned to face Annie. 'But don't you think you should just let this Damien thing die a natural death? You know what they say about other fish in the sea. There are some okay guys at my work—'

'This isn't just about Damien,' Annie said quickly. 'It's about me. I want to sort it out. I don't want to be left up in the air until Damien eventually decides to turn up.'

Mel gave a puzzled shrug.

From near the front door Victoria called, 'You ready, Mel?'

'Yeah, coming.' To Annie, she said, 'You do what you like, Annie, but I think you might be out of luck. The university year will be winding down now. Lectures will have finished and the students will be on swot vacation getting ready for exams.'

'Oh.'

As Mel hurried for the door she called over her shoulder, 'If I were you, I'd stick to shopping.'

'No, thank you,' Annie said quietly.

When a knock sounded on his office door Theo Grainger was deep in a mire of student assignments and he grunted a greeting without looking up from the papers on his desk.

'Dr Grainger?'

He'd assumed that Lillian, the philosophy department's receptionist, was dropping off the day's mail. But this voice wasn't Lillian's; it was younger, no doubt a student panicking about forthcoming exams.

He didn't bother to raise his head. 'Do you have an appointment?' he asked just a little too gruffly.

'No.'

His aggrieved sigh drifted downwards to the pile of papers on his desk. 'You must know by now that all students have to make an appointment to see me. Put your name against a time slot on the notice board.'

'All right.'

He returned to the assignment he was grading—a rather badly constructed analysis of utilitarianism.

'One problem,' the voice at the door said. 'Could you please tell me where the notice board is?'

Theo's head snapped up and he glared at the caller. 'How long have you been a student here?'

'No time at all.' Her mouth twisted into an apologetic smile and she pushed a wing of blonde hair back behind her ear. 'You see, I'm not a student.'

The surprise of recognition startled him like a bolt from the blue.

Annie McKinnon.

Just in time, he stopped himself from saying her name aloud. The last thing he wanted was

for her to realise that he'd seen her before—
that he'd been watching her—virtually spying
on her yesterday evening.

He rose slowly to his feet. 'I'm sorry,' he
said. 'What did you say your name was?'

'I didn't actually get my name out. I must
be nervous.' She gave a self-conscious roll of
her eyes. 'I'm almost ashamed to admit it, but
I'm Annie McKinnon.' She winced. 'You answered an email I sent to your nephew,
Damien.'

'Ah, yes.' Theo knew it was unkind, but he
couldn't resist tipping his head forward to ap-
praise Annie with a searching look over the top
of his spectacles.

Not surprisingly, she squirmed.

'So,' he said. 'I have the pleasure of meeting
the forthright Miss McKinnon.'

'I'm sorry, Dr Grainger. If my friends and I
had known *you* were going to read that email
we wouldn't have been so—so forthright.'

'I can well believe that.' Theo was still
holding the pen he'd been using to mark the
students' assignments. Now, he replaced its lid
and set it carefully back on his desk. When he
looked at Annie again he felt as if she'd been
staring at him intensely. He offered her a cautious smile. 'So why did you want to see me?'

She returned his slow smile measure for cautious measure. 'I wanted to apologise to you.'

'I'm not sure that *you* need to apologise.'

'Well, I also wanted to find out the truth.'

'The truth?'

'About Damien.'

Her gaze locked with his and she stopped smiling. Her eyes were clear blue—the kind of blue that made Theo think of summer sky reflected in spring water, and it occurred to him that their astonishing candour must be an Annie McKinnon trademark.

Standing straight as a soldier, she said, 'I need to know if Damien was really called away on urgent business, or if he simply didn't want to meet me.'

Theo cleared his throat. After observing this young woman last night, he should have known that she wouldn't simply turn tail and give up. 'Perhaps we should discuss this somewhere else,' he said and he glanced at his watch. Best to get her safely away from the curious eyes and ears of his colleagues and departmental secretaries. 'Let me buy you coffee.'

'Thank you,' she said warmly. 'That would be wonderful.'

Seeing the sudden animated brightness in

her face, Theo wasn't so sure. He lifted a navy-blue blazer from the back of his chair and shrugged his shoulders into it, then he gestured for her to accompany him down the hallway. It was a warm November day and the formality of the blazer was unnecessary, but it gave Theo a sense of protection and, for some peculiar reason, a glowing, excited Annie McKinnon at his side called for protection.

Their journey took them through the Philosophy department's reception area and Lillian looked up from her desk.

Annie smiled and waved to her. 'I found him,' she called gleefully.

Lillian returned Annie's wave, and then her amused eyes met Theo's. They glimmered with undeniable curiosity and one eyebrow rose, but Theo hurried forward, eager to get his nephew's jilted girlfriend out of the building.

Wow.

As she walked with Theo Grainger through the Great Court of the University of Queensland, Annie was seriously impressed.

Talk about hallowed halls. With its stretch of green lawn encircled by graceful columns and arches, the courtyard was as dignified and atmospheric as any place she'd ever seen. And all the surrounding buildings were made out of beautiful sandstone, too. As she looked around at their impressive façades she felt a sense of awe.

She could almost smell knowledge in the air. How could anyone *not* become earnest and clever in this inspiring environment?

'Do these people have any idea how lucky they are to be here?' she said, casting an envious eye over the students strolling casually past.

Theo smiled. 'Not enough of them, I'm afraid.' He turned to her. 'So you didn't have the chance to go to university?'

'I was planning to go straight after boarding school, but then my father died and things kind of fell apart at home. I live on a cattle station up in North Queensland—so I stayed home for a year, and after that it was just assumed that I would stay on indefinitely.'

'But that wasn't your plan?'

'I didn't mind at first, but in the past few years I've been champing at the bit.'

'It's never too late to start at university.'

'That's what I've been thinking. Twenty-four's still quite young really, isn't it?'

'Very young,' he said in an ambiguous tone that puzzled her.

They reached a café in a leafy garden setting

and Theo collected two white coffees and carried them to a secluded table, away from chattering students.

They both opened slim paper sachets of sugar, used half, then twisted the unused halves and set them on their saucers. Annie laughed. 'We could have shared a sugar if we'd known we only wanted half each.'

Theo looked surprised, then smiled and shook his head as if he didn't quite know what to make of her.

Well, that made two of them. She was certainly feeling shocked and unsure about Damien's Uncle Theo. He wasn't *anything* like she'd expected.

She'd had an image in her mind of an absent-minded professor type—a badly groomed academic, aged fifty plus, carelessly dressed in a wrinkled shirt and rumpled trousers. She'd expected untidy hair, a beard perhaps, and most definitely a scowl.

But although this man had scowled at her when she first knocked on his door, he'd quickly become polite. And heck, he couldn't be older than her brothers, who were in their mid-thirties.

As for his appearance—his grooming was impeccable. Neat, dark hair, crisp blue shirt and stone-coloured trousers. Tall, trim physique. His dark-rimmed glasses gave his hazel eyes a scholarly air, but in no way did they detract from his appearance.

But he was a philosopher, for heaven's sake.

Somehow she hadn't expected someone so painfully thoughtful and clever to look quite so—so worldly. He was actually very *attractive*. But in a way that was refreshingly different from the tough ringers and jackaroos she was used to in the outback.

Then again, perhaps Theo's appearance shouldn't really surprise her since he was related by blood to Damien.

Thinking of Damien, she felt suddenly subdued, and she picked up her coffee and took a sip while she considered the best way to ask this man about his nephew.

'It's very kind of you to take time out to see me,' she said as she placed the cup back in its saucer. 'You must think I'm very foolish really, trying to arrange a date over the Internet.'

'If you're foolish, then so are thousands of other people.' He sent her a reassuring smile. 'Dating on the Internet is becoming more popular every day.'

'Well, thanks. That makes me feel a bit better.'

'But I'm sorry you've come such a long

way. And it's a pity you feel let down by Damien.'

'I have a right to feel let down, don't I?'

'Everyone has a right to their feelings.'

Annie frowned at him. 'I have a horrible feeling right now that you're going to start philosophising and I'll get lost. Can you just tell me straight? Is Damien avoiding me?'

He sighed and dropped his gaze to stare hard at his coffee. 'I'm not sure.'

'You must have a fair idea.'

At that he looked up and the glimmer of a smile sparked in his eyes. 'Have you ever thought of becoming a prosecuting attorney, Miss McKinnon?'

'Why?'

'You have a disturbingly direct manner. I defy anyone to lie to you.'

'Good,' she said quickly. Their gazes met across the table and for a moment she almost lost her train of thought. Drawing a quick breath, she said, 'Does that mean you're going to drop the Miss McKinnon and call me Annie and tell me the truth? Damien's a jerk, isn't he?'

'If you've already made up your mind, I don't need to answer that.' Theo paused, then added softly, 'Annie.'

When he pronounced her name in his lovely

deep, educated voice the strangest shiver ran through her. She felt as if she'd been tapped on the shoulder, as if an unheard voice had whispered something important in her ear.

The feeling was so distinct that for a moment she had to close her eyes. When she opened them again, Theo Grainger was watching her and she saw a puzzling tension in his expression.

'Please,' she said softly, feeling strangely shaken. 'Don't play mind games with me. Just tell me, so I can put this whole mess behind me.'

He sighed and pushed his half-empty coffee cup to one side so that he could rest his clasped hands on the table in front of him. 'I honestly don't know Damien's exact reasons for getting out of the city this week, but I'm afraid he was anxious to avoid your date. I'm sorry. My nephew doesn't have a very good track record. He's prone to pranks and he's managed to upset quite a few people one way or another.'

'I see.' She drank some more of her coffee.

'I hope you're not too heartbroken.'

Strange, but she wasn't nearly as upset as she thought she'd be. The news that she was the victim of some kind of prank no longer surprised her. It was more like receiving confirmation of something she'd suspected in theory, but hadn't tested in practice. *Yes, Annie, fire will burn you.*

Damien's uncle was expecting a response from her. She looked at him. 'I can assure you, Dr Grainger, it will take something much worse than being stood up on a blind date before I allow my heart to be broken.'

For a moment he looked startled. 'That's a relief,' he said.

But he didn't look particularly relieved and they both turned quickly to stare over to the distant Brisbane River. Annie watched the slow drift of the water as she finished her coffee.

'Actually, there is *something* I'm very upset about,' she said.

'What's that?'

'I won't get to meet Basil.'

'Basil?'

She turned back to him. 'Damien's dog. His Dalmatian.'

'Is that what he told you? That he has a Dalmatian called Basil?'

'Yes.' She leaned towards him, eager to make her point. 'It was part of the reason we clicked. I'm mad about dogs. Damien and I used to joke about how fabulous it would be if my Border collie, Lavender, fell in love with his Basil. I know it sounds childish, but it was fun. We used to say that if Basil and Lavender mated we would have a pot-pourri of puppies.'

Theo smiled briefly, then frowned and shook his head.

Annie slumped in her chair. 'Don't tell me that's a lie, too. I couldn't bear it if Basil doesn't exist.'

'Oh, don't worry, Basil most certainly exists,' he said quietly. 'But he's *my* dog.'

CHAPTER THREE

'How long would it take me to walk from here to the Goodwill Bridge?' Annie asked Mel, who was in the middle of brushing her teeth before bed.

To her relief, Mel and Victoria had opted for an early night this evening.

Mel turned from the sink. 'Oh, I'd say about half an hour. Why?'

'I want to set my alarm.'

Lowering her toothbrush, Mel frowned at her. 'You're going to walk to the Goodwill Bridge tomorrow morning?'

'Yes.'

'Why on earth would you want to do that?'

'I want to go for an early morning walk and that bridge will take me over the river to the South Bank, won't it?'

'Yes, Annie, but I thought you came to Brisbane for fun, not exercise.'

Annie shrugged. 'A little exercise won't hurt me.' She turned to leave the bathroom. 'Goodnight.'

'Hang on,' Mel called, making a hurried effort to rinse her mouth.

With some reluctance, Annie paused in the hallway. She'd been hoping to avoid an inquisition about this.

Mel came through the doorway, still wiping her mouth with the back of her hand. 'Okay, confession time! You didn't come to the city for a health kick, so who are you going to meet on the bridge?'

Annie sighed extravagantly. 'A dog. A Dalmatian dog called Basil.'

'Oh, yeah?' Mel let her eyes roll towards the ceiling. 'And will Basil be waiting for you all by himself? He doesn't, by any chance, come attached to some yummy guy you've met today, does he?'

'Theo will be there,' Annie mumbled.

'Who?'

'Theo.'

'Theo?' Mel's voice rose an octave. 'Theo as in Dr Theo Grainger?'

'Yes.' In defence Annie added, 'I told you I spoke to him this morning. And he's invited me to meet his dog.'

Mel collapsed against the wall in helpless laughter.

'What's the big joke? You know I'm nuts about dogs.'

'Oh, yeah, sure, Annie. You're fascinated by Theo Grainger's dog. But *hello*—half the UQ philosophy undergraduates are nuts about Dr Theo.'

Annie couldn't hide her surprise.

'The female half, that is,' Mel amended. 'Not that it gets them anywhere. Apparently, he has a policy of never dating students.'

'Good for him.'

'But that's why I'm so gobsmacked. How did you wangle this date with him?'

'For crying out loud, Mel. Walking a dog is *not* a date.'

'Yeah?' Smiling, Mel shook her head. 'That's like saying a foot massage has nothing to do with sex.'

To her dismay, Annie found it difficult to meet her friend's gaze.

There was an awkward silence while she stared at the floor and then Mel said more gently, 'Well, don't worry. We'll just have to keep our fingers crossed that jerkishness doesn't run in Damien's family.'

Impulsive decisions often had unpleasant repercussions, Theo reminded himself the next morning as he waited at the northern end of the Goodwill Bridge and watched the blue and white City Cats ferrying passengers up and down the Brisbane River.

He suspected that the impulse to invite Annie McKinnon to join him on a walk with his dog had been foolish. But she'd been badly misled by his nephew and he consoled himself that his sense of obligation to her was a worthy motivation.

After spending almost a decade as a university lecturer, he was well aware of the pitfalls of offering even the most casual friendship to an attractive young woman. But in Annie's case it should be quite a simple matter to guard against repercussions.

He'd kept the invitation very low-key. He'd even been ungallant enough to let her find her own way to the bridge, but now he wondered if she might get lost.

He switched his attention from the river to the traffic speeding to join the network of concrete ribbons that formed the freeway system and in his peripheral vision he caught sight of a hand waving.

Annie.

She was waiting at the pedestrian crossing on the other side of the road. The lights changed and within less than a minute she came hurrying up to him.

'I hope I'm not too late,' she said, panting slightly, as if she'd been running.

'Not at all.'

She dropped to her knees, and focused her attention entirely on the dog. 'Oh, Basil, you're beautiful. I could recognise your gorgeous black and white spots when I was still a block away.'

She ruffled Basil's ears and made a great fuss of him and Theo tried not to notice the way her hair shone in the sun, or how slim and lithe she looked in her black shorts and sleeveless pale blue top. He turned quickly to study the clusters of apartment block towers built close to the river.

'So which way are we going?' she asked, jumping to her feet.

'Over the bridge. Ready?'

'Sure.'

The Goodwill Bridge was restricted to pedestrians and cyclists and as they set off across its gentle arc the city buzzed around them. At this early hour the air was still and cool, the sky clear, and the parks and gardens green. Brisbane looked clean and at its best.

'Hey, Theo, is that Italian writing on your T-shirt?'

Annie had the most disturbing way of asking unexpected questions. 'Yes,' he admitted, looking down at the slogan on his chest. 'It's an ad for coffee.'

'Can you read Italian? Do you know what it says?'

'It's something like… For people who really care about the coffee they drink.'

She looked excessively impressed. 'Have you ever been to Italy?'

'Yes, many times.'

'Wow, I'd give anything to see Rome or Venice or Florence. I've read all I can about them and I drool over the pictures.'

'Italy's beautiful. I think it's my favourite European country.'

'Really?'

To his surprise she looked puzzled.

'You have a problem with that?'

'No, it's just that it's Damien's favourite country too.'

'But he's never been to Italy.'

She came to a sudden halt and Theo tugged on Basil's lead. 'Hang on, boy.'

'This is weird,' she said. 'Do you think Damien has been pretending to be someone like you?'

'I can't think why. What makes you think so? Because of the dog and Italy?'

'Not only that.' She turned to look out at the river where an old wooden ferry was chugging from one side to the other. 'He used to tell me things about philosophy, too.'

Theo laughed. 'Philosophy? Damien doesn't know the first thing about philosophy.'

'Well, he sounded knowledgeable to me.' She turned back and offered him a sheepish smile. 'But then I wouldn't have a clue. I'm more of an old movie fan. As far as I know, Scarlett O'Hara's ''Tomorrow is another day'' could be philosophy.'

'And you wouldn't be too far off the mark.'

She shook her head. 'I'm beginning to feel so stupid about this. I can't believe all the things I lov—liked about Damien were all make-believe.'

Not make-believe, Theo thought. They were me.

Annie's china-blue eyes were round with worry and when their gazes met she chewed her lip and colour stained her neck and cheeks. Had the same idea occurred to her?

When Damien came back he would strangle him.

She let out a long sigh, then shrugged. 'I've got to stop talking about Damien. I'm over him. Let's keep walking. I didn't mean to hold you up.'

They walked on and Annie's gaze darted everywhere, her hungry eyes taking in the towering buildings, the busy traffic on the freeway and the boats on the river. She looked as if she'd never seen anything quite so exciting.

He'd noticed the same sense of delighted engagement with her surroundings at the university yesterday, and now he tried unsuccessfully to suppress the thought that the clever, academic women he'd dated in recent years were a bunch of jaded cynics.

They reached the other side of the bridge and he looked below to the dry dock where volunteers were restoring an ancient tugboat. He'd been taking a keen interest in their progress.

'Oh, look at that.' Annie was pointing ahead to a forest of very modern unit buildings surrounded by landscaped gardens and restaurants.

'What are you looking at?'

'That dear little clock tower peeping over the fig trees.'

'Oh, yes. It's part of the old South Brisbane Town Hall. It's very Victorian, isn't it?'

'Yes, it's all red-bricked and old-fashioned and out of place, but it's gorgeous,' she said. 'I'm sure it disapproves of all these modern aluminium and glass buildings.'

'Just like the old Queen would have.'

'Exactly!' Annie laughed and her hair

glinted pale gold in the sunlight and, without warning, she flung her arms skywards and executed a three hundred and sixty degree spin. 'Oh, I lo-o-o-ve this city!'

And bang went Theo's resolve to remain aloof.

'Would you like to stop for breakfast?' he asked.

Breakfast? Annie bit back a cry of surprise. Come to think of it, Theo was looking surprised too. Perhaps he'd realised that adding breakfast to a walk along the river turned the occasion into something that was almost a date. Maybe he was having second thoughts.

She wondered if she should let him off the hook.

But she didn't want to. Something happened to her whenever she was with him. Something deep. Elusive. Nagging.

And it had nothing to do with his dog, and only a little to do with how great he looked in athletic shorts.

'What about our casual clothes?'

'Don't worry. Most of the eateries along here cater to walkers and joggers.'

'What about Basil, then? He won't be allowed in a restaurant, will he?'

'A friend of mine owns one of the cafés on

the riverfront and on special occasions he's happy to keep him out the back for me, away from the kitchen and the diners.'

'Does this count as a special occasion?'

He smiled slowly. 'If I say so.

His smile made her chest grow tight. She bent down and scratched Basil's spotty head. 'Do you mind being tied up, beautiful boy?'

Basil's tail wagged madly and Theo said, 'Giovanni spoils him so much he never minds.'

'Looks like we're having breakfast, then.'

Annie wondered if her heart had burst into song as they walked through a colonnade of purple bougainvillea. Time to calm down. *This is not a date. This is not a date.*

They turned on to the wide walkway close to the river, where cafés and restaurants were already doing a busy breakfast trade.

A rotund, balding Italian turned from adjusting a red and white striped umbrella over a table. When he saw them his face split into an enormous grin and he called in a booming voice, '*Ciao*, Theo.'

'Giovanni! *Ciao.*'

The men exchanged backslaps as they chatted in Italian. Annie watched, enchanted. Giovanni grinned at her too.

'*Buon giorno, signora.*'

Oh, wow. I'm melting. No one had ever called her *signora* and it sounded sensational in Giovanni's Italian baritone. Warming. Like brandy slipping through her veins.

'*Buon giorno*, Giovanni,' she said back to him. Her pronunciation didn't sound quite right, but nevertheless he looked delighted.

Theo looked pleased with her too.

Almost immediately, Giovanni took hold of Basil's lead. '*È un cane bello*,' he said, giving the dog a pat with his massive hand. Then he waved to them both as he disappeared with Basil around the back of the café.

'That's Basil settled,' said Theo. 'Now, let's find a table.'

Annie could hardly contain her excitement as they sat at a table for two overlooking the water. Breakfast by the Brisbane River with a view of skyscrapers and the busy freeway— she felt so urban and classy.

Okay, this wasn't a date, but La Piastra was Dullsville by comparison.

'What are you going to have?' she asked Theo as they studied their menus.

'I think I'll settle for something light. Probably a sourdough bagel and coffee.'

She wondered what her brothers would think of a man who ate a bagel for breakfast. At home, Reid and Kane expected steak and eggs and a mountain of toast. But they headed off to a day of hard physical work, of course. Most likely Theo would be sitting at a desk.

'I can't decide between a croissant or fruit toast,' she said.

'The fruit toast is very good. Especially if you like dried figs.'

'Oh, yum. No contest then. Fruit toast it is.'

'And coffee?'

'Yes, please.' At Southern Cross she always had tea, but here in the city her taste buds were primed for coffee. Just the smell of it was sophisticated.

Once their orders were placed, Theo leaned back in his chair and looked up at the sky. He seemed relaxed. In a good mood.

Prepared to talk?

Annie took a deep breath. 'Do you mind if I ask you a nosy question?'

Behind his glasses his eyes narrowed slightly, but he didn't look annoyed. His mouth tilted into a slow smile. 'That's difficult to answer without knowing the question.'

'Okay, I'll ask it and you don't have to answer if you don't want to.'

Theo nodded. 'Fair enough.'

'It's just that I feel so ignorant. I've been wondering what philosophers actually do.'

'Ah… I should have seen that coming.'

'Sorry,' she said quickly. 'Do a lot of people ask you that?'

'Just about everyone.'

'Ouch. It's just that I can't imagine you just sit and think clever thoughts all day long. You must—' She broke off, suddenly out of her depth.

'You think we must find *something* useful to do?' he suggested.

'I didn't mean to be insulting. I suppose I'm asking this because your life is so different from *mine*. Where I live, people have to be practical. They have no choice. If a bore breaks down they can't sit around waiting for someone to travel hundreds of kilometres to fix it.'

'And philosophers don't build things or grow things or fix things.'

'I don't know. Do you?'

Theo crossed his arms over his chest. And Annie felt a stab of alarm. Hadn't the girls warned her that this was a very negative sign in body language?

'Obviously philosophers don't bake bagels or build skyscrapers or fix bores,' he said.

The waiter arrived with their breakfast and she was relieved to be diverted by delicious thick slices of toast, heavy with fruit. She was happy to drop the subject of Theo's job, especially if he was touchy about it.

He held up a sachet of sugar and smiled at her.

'Want to share?' he asked.

Oh, crumbs, he had such a nice smile. 'Sure.' She grinned back at him and hoped that their awkward moment was behind them.

But as he spread cream cheese on his bagel Theo said, 'Philosophers build things.'

She nodded and popped a piece of toast into her mouth, trying to look casually interested, but not wanting him to feel pressured into further explanation.

'They work out structures for thinking,' he went on. 'And, once you've got those structures in place, you can think through all sorts of problems more easily. But it's not just a matter of mental gymnastics. Philosophers make connections to real life. These days philosophy is being used more and more as therapy.'

'Like in counselling?'

'Yes. Some people find a thoughtful dose of Aristotle or Plato can be more useful than medication.'

'Wow, that sounds really interesting. I could probably do with a dose of philosophy. People are always telling me I'm too impulsive and don't think things through before I act.' She traced the handle of her coffee cup with her finger. 'There's so much I don't know.'

'Nobody can know what they haven't yet experienced.'

'I guess not.' Her eyes met his. 'But I'd like to be wise, especially about things that really matter.'

Theo didn't answer immediately. He cut a piece of bagel, but before he ate it he looked at her and said gently, 'You might be wiser than you think, Annie. Plato decided that his own wisdom lay in realizing how little he knew about the things that matter most.'

A breeze danced across the river and picked up strands of Annie's hair and tossed them on to her face. As she fingered them back into place Theo stared at her arm, frowning.

Bending her elbow to examine it, she saw the purple smudge of bruises. 'I got these from sleeping on Mel's couch,' she explained. 'It's so narrow and lumpy I keep rolling off and I banged my elbow on the coffee table. I suppose I'll have more bruises by the end of the week.'

'Sounds uncomfortable.'

'Yeah. If I'd known how bad it was I would have brought my camp swag and slept on the floor. Mind you, I didn't give Mel much warn-

ing that I was coming and she's been very ac-
commodating.'

He looked thoughtful as he drank his coffee.

Annie checked her watch. 'How much time
do you have? Don't you need to go to work?'

'Yes, I do, but now lectures have finished I
can be a little more flexible with my schedule.'
He set down his coffee cup. 'Just the same, I'd
better get going.'

'Basil will be restless.'

'Either that or he will have gone to sleep,
with a tummy full of the best off-cuts of
Giovanni's fillet steak.'

Breakfast over, Theo attended to the bill,
and they collected Basil and set off again along
the South Bank walkway.

'What do you plan to do with the rest of
your week in the city?'

Darn. Annie wished he hadn't asked that.

'You're *what*?' Mel dropped the knife she'd
been using to slice mushrooms. Her hands flew
to her hips as she almost shouted her question
at Annie.

Victoria, who was perched on a kitchen
stool and chopping carrots, looked equally
stunned.

Annie hastened to appease them. 'It's not
that I don't appreciate how generous you've

both been, letting me use your couch, and you've been wonderful helping me with the clothes shopping and the date with Damien and everything. I'm very grateful.'

'But I can't believe you're moving in with Dr Grainger,' said Mel.

Victoria shook her head. 'Why would you want to move in with some stuffy old philosopher who's related to the jerk?'

'It's because Theo *is* Damien's uncle that he's offered me Damien's room for the rest of my time here,' Annie explained. 'He feels a sense of obligation.'

Mel hooted. 'Obligation? Is that what he calls it? I reckon he's feeling something much more physical that ends with "tion".'

'Perhaps you're being a tad naïve,' suggested Victoria.

Annie groaned. How could she explain Theo's invitation without making reference to the girls' narrow couch and the bruises?

'I promise you, this is a very platonic arrangement,' she said.

'Listen to her.' Mel winked at Victoria. 'She's had breakfast with a philosopher and already she's throwing around words like platonic.'

'Give me a break, please!'

Annie hadn't meant to shout, but it worked.

Mel and Victoria's mouths snapped shut. In unison, they crossed their arms over their chests.

She took a deep breath. 'I thought this was a good idea for several reasons. Number one, you get your couch back.' When Mel opened her mouth, she signalled her to shush. 'Number two, Damien's caused me grief and I may as well enjoy the comfort of his room while he's not using it.' She hurried on. 'Number three, Theo's house is within walking distance of the art gallery and the library, the theatres, and the South Bank. It's a really handy location for me to entertain myself during the day.'

'What about the nights?' came Victoria's predictable response.

Annie swallowed. 'Theo's not going to pounce on me, if that's what you're worried about. He's a gentleman.'

'But he's also rather gorgeous,' said Mel. 'Have you considered the fact that you might fall for him and get hurt all over again?'

'Like nephew, like uncle,' chanted Victoria in a singsong voice.

Suddenly there was silence. Annie avoided their eyes. She knew Mel had a point. There was a very good chance that she was already rather smitten by Theo Grainger and it was unlikely that he was interested in her romantically, so no doubt there was an element of risk.

But then again...her instincts were screaming for her to accept Theo's invitation. To start with, she knew now that the man she'd foolishly fallen in love with over the Internet was more Theo than he was ever Damien. Why Damien had taken his uncle's persona was a mystery. But it was only part of a much bigger mystery now.

When she and Theo were together something happened. She wasn't sure what it was exactly. It was so tenuous and fragile and unexpected that she couldn't give it an obvious name. But she felt its pull and she found it irresistibly thrilling.

'I'm prepared to take that risk,' she said.

Mel's eyes widened in horror. 'Oh, no. You've fallen for him already, haven't you?'

'No! I don't know him well enough for that.'

'Hang on,' broke in Victoria. 'Why would she fall for this uncle? How can he be gorgeous? Isn't he ancient?'

Mel shook her head. 'At a guess, I'd say mid-thirties.'

Victoria's jaw dropped. She stared at Annie and then her face softened into a knowing smile. 'Go, Annie,' she said quietly, her voice rippling with undertone.

'Well, that's that then,' said Mel. 'It looks like Victoria's on your side, Annie. Two against one. So I bow out of this debate.' She heaved a dramatic sigh. 'But you'd better ring your brothers and explain your plans. Reid left a message on our answering machine today and he sounded pretty worried. I'm certainly not prepared to tell him what you're up to.'

'Yes, of course. I'll ring him now.'

'I'm surprised he didn't catch you on your mobile.'

'Um...he might have. I switched it off and I haven't checked for messages.'

Mel's eyebrows rose. 'Been a touch distracted, have we?' Annie didn't reply. Her decision to turn her phone off had been deliberate. Reid and Kane were probably mad at her for running away to the city and she hadn't felt ready to field their calls.

'Well, Annie,' Mel said. 'If your bags are packed, we can drive you over to the south side as soon as we've had dinner.'

Crossing the kitchen quickly, Annie gave her a hug. 'Thanks for everything, Mel. I don't know what I'd do without friends like you and Victoria. But you don't have to give me a lift. I don't mind getting a taxi.'

'No way,' cut in Victoria. 'Apart from the fact that Mel won't rest easy until she's seen you safely delivered, you can't deny us the chance to see where this mystery uncle lives. We might even get a peek at the great man himself.' She caught the expression in Annie's eyes and added, 'Don't worry, I promise not to embarrass you.'

Tummy churning strangely, Annie went into the lounge room to ring her brothers before collecting her belongings. Not sure where on the huge property they might be, she dialled the number of their satellite phone. Reid answered.

'Annie, thank God it's you. I've rung half of Brisbane trying to track you down.'

She felt instantly contrite. 'I'm sorry. I've been meaning to ring you. How are you?'

'Much better now that I'm hearing your voice and know you're alive.' After a beat, he added, 'I had my fingers crossed that no news meant good news. You must be having a good time.'

'Yes, I am—a wonderful time, but I must admit I've been feeling guilty about taking off the way I did without warning you or Kane.'

'Well—to be totally honest I can't really blame you, Annie. Kane and I both tend to take you for granted and we chauvinist types deserve a bit of a shake up now and again. And *you* deserve some fun in the city if that's what you're hankering for.'

Dear old Reid. In her heart of hearts, Annie had known he would understand.

'So how long will you be staying at Melissa's?' he asked.

'A-ah—' Annie gulped. She spoke slowly while her mind raced. 'I'm not actually staying at Melissa's place any more. I'm moving to another—friend's place for a few days. There's more room there and it's closer to the galleries and the theatre and everything, so it's terrific. But you'll still be able to reach me on this mobile number. How's everything at home?'

'Lavender's missing you like crazy. She's taken to moping again.'

'Oh, the poor darling.' Instantly she saw a picture of her Border collie, lying in a dispirited sprawl on the back veranda at Southern Cross with her head slumped across her paws. 'Please give her an extra hug from me.'

'I'm afraid I can't. I'm not at home. I've had to come over to Lacey Downs because Mary Rogers went into premature labour.'

'Oh, no. Is everything all right?'

'She's fine now. Had a baby girl.'

'Lovely. She was hoping for a girl.'

'I'll be out here for a week or so.'

Annie grimaced guiltily. 'Sounds like I picked a bad time to take off. Maybe I should come home?' She crossed her fingers, hoping that Reid would say no. She couldn't bear to go home now.

'No, it's okay. Kane's found an English girl to help out at Southern Cross.'

She tried not to sound too relieved. 'That was handy.'

'Yeah.' Reid paused. 'I hope he knows what he's doing.'

The doubt in his voice caused her a twinge of concern, but she decided not to question Reid too closely about Kane and the English girl. It might prompt him to change his mind and say that she was needed at home or, worse still, he might put some more questions to her about her new accommodation.

'I'll have a better idea of my plans in a few days time,' she assured him. 'I'll ring next week and let you know.'

'Okay. Have fun, little sis.'

'Thanks, big brother. I will. Love you, Reid.'

'Love you too, chicken. Take care now.'

It was only after she'd disconnected that she thought again about Kane and the English girl, alone together now at Southern Cross. Why had Reid sounded concerned? It wasn't like him to make a fuss over nothing.

But all thoughts of Kane were banished when Victoria suddenly dashed into the room. 'He's here,' she hissed. 'He's at the front door now.'

Annie's heart rocked. 'Who?' she asked, knowing that there could really only be one answer.

'The uncle. Cripes, Annie, you didn't tell me your philosopher was a hunk. I have never seen glasses make a man look so sexy. *And* he drives a silver convertible with a Dalmatian in the back!'

'Does he?' Annie squeaked. 'I told him not to bother picking me up. I—'

'Didn't want us to be jealous when we saw him?' asked Victoria. 'Oh, baby, I can't blame you.'

CHAPTER FOUR

As Theo drove Annie back across the river to his place, he steeled himself to remain immune to her infectious enthusiasm.

His plan was solid. He would be the perfect gentleman, friendly but reserved. Yes, he would play the role of an attentive host while maintaining an avuncular distance from her. It should be easy enough given the gap in their ages and their backgrounds.

The only wild card in his tidy scheme was Annie herself. She had an unnerving knack for throwing him off guard.

As soon as they arrived at his town house he carried her bag straight up to the second floor where the bedrooms were, and set it on a rug just inside the doorway of Damien's room.

She stepped into the room and looked around at the double bed covered with a plain navy bedspread, and the glass topped table beside it. 'Damien's very neat and tidy.'

'His room looks a little bare because I asked

Mrs Feather, who cleans for me, to tidy away the clutter of Damien's personal things.'

'She did a great job.'

Indeed. Perhaps Mrs Feather had followed his instructions just a little too conscientiously. The room did look unnaturally austere. The only ornaments were the lamp on the bedside table and a novelty alarm clock shaped like a television set.

The computer on the pine desk in the corner was switched off and covered with a plastic protector. The timber shutters were drawn across the windows and the walls were completely bare, although Theo could see faint marks where posters of pop groups had hung.

'You have your own *en suite* bathroom. It's through there,' he said, pointing to a doorway. 'So you'll be quite private.'

'That's wonderful. Thank you.'

She lifted her arms to run her fingers through her wind-tousled hair and the movement made her top separate from her jeans to reveal a section of her midriff. Theo saw a couple of inches of smooth, soft skin, and the curve of an exceptionally feminine hip bone and slender waist.

'I'll be down in the kitchen,' he said, backing towards the doorway. 'Do you like mussels?'

She turned, her blue eyes shining with amusement. 'Muscles?'

'The shellfish.'

'Oh, I don't know. I don't think I've ever eaten them, but I'll try anything once.'

'Do you usually like seafood?'

'Yes, I love it.'

'Then mussels should be fine.'

She frowned. 'You're not cooking them, are you?'

'Yes.' He shrugged to make light of it. 'Don't you trust me?'

'But I should be doing the cooking. Heck, Theo, you go to work all day and you've given me this lovely accommodation. The least I can do is cook. Mind you, most of the recipes I'm used to have beef in them.'

He smiled. 'Another night, perhaps.'

When Theo left, Annie took her toiletry bag through to the neat little bathroom and washed her face and brushed the tangles from her hair, caused by the windy but thrilling drive in Theo's convertible. She thought about adding a touch of lipstick, but decided against it. At home she hardly ever wore make-up and she felt uncomfortable using it unless she was all dolled up for a special occasion.

Besides, she didn't want Theo to think she

was trying too hard to impress him. She would unpack later, she decided. She felt a little uncomfortable in Damien's too neat room and she was keen to check out the rest of the house.

On the way to the stairs she passed Theo's bedroom. The last of the twilight was pooling through open floor-to-ceiling timber shutters on to a rich cream bedspread and an artistic tumble of black and cream cushions. His king-size bed was framed by carved timber posts. All sorts of books were piled on one of the matching side tables.

She looked at the sumptuous bed and pictured it at night, looking even more sumptuous in the glow cast by the impressive bedside lamps with heavy gold bases and black shades... But then she pictured Theo in the bed...and she wanted to put herself in the picture, too.

As if...

She hurried downstairs.

Theo's kitchen was at the back of the ground floor section of his narrow town house and as she made her way through the living area she couldn't help admiring his taste in interior decor.

The furnishings were similar to his bedroom—masculine colours like charcoal grey, black and cream that blended wonderfully with the honeyed tones of the polished timber floors and the floor-to-ceiling timber bookshelves. One wall was painted dark red, and set against it were abstract black and white paintings in thick gold frames.

Music drifted from the kitchen—a rhythmic drumbeat, a thrumming guitar and the alluring, smoky voice of one of her favourite Gypsy singers—another passion she'd thought she'd shared with Damien.

And there was a sensational aroma wafting through the house. She sniffed the air, trying to identify the ingredients and decided that it was lemon and crushed garlic and a herb, perhaps parsley, being heated in olive oil. Then she walked into Theo's kitchen and it was like walking into another world.

To start with, Theo was at the stove.

For a girl who'd grown up in the McKinnon household, where a man only stepped up to a kitchen stove in a dire emergency, it was a remarkable sight, especially as Theo looked convincingly masculine and yet so totally at home with a striped tea towel draped over one broad shoulder while he stirred something in a heavy enamel pot.

But the music and the smells enchanted her, too…

And then the room itself...gleaming white walls and smart black granite bench tops...a white platter piled with lemons, and elegant wrought iron stools pulled up to a tall bench...sliding doors leading to a leafy courtyard strung with tiny lights. And a table set for two.

'This is almost ready,' Theo said over his shoulder. 'I have a nice white wine chilled. Would you like some?'

He turned and smiled at her.

And Annie feared she might actually swoon.

The mussels were as delicious as they smelled. Theo served them in their shells, accompanied by linguini, which he'd tossed in a simple sauce made from tomatoes and basil leaves. The meal had an uncomplicated, direct combination of flavours that Annie loved and she couldn't resist licking her lips.

'Does this dish have a name?' she asked.

'*Spaghetti della Paulo*.'

'And what does that mean?'

'That it's Paulo's recipe. He's a restaurateur who lives in Rome. I met him on one of my trips to Italy.'

'I should have guessed that,' she said, smiling. 'Wow! I suppose you'd never need to go to La Piastra.'

'On the contrary, it's one of my favourite restaurants.'

Of course.

There it was again. The unnerving connection between Damien and Theo that she tried not to think about.

She glanced down at Basil, lying at their feet as they dined in the courtyard, then she sipped some wine.

'Tell me a little about your home at Southern Cross,' said Theo. 'I'm sure my understanding of life on a cattle station is very romanticised. I hardly know anything about what happens on a day to day basis.'

Annie shrugged. 'It depends on the time of the year. In the mustering season it's fun to get out in the bush for weeks at a time, sleeping in swags under the stars. But at other times it's pretty routine. There's always general maintenance work—fixing fences, checking water, putting out feed supplements.'

He asked more questions, surprising her with his eagerness to hear details about these tasks and other aspects of handling stock. Then he looked thoughtful for a moment. 'It's ages since I've slept under the stars.'

'You should come to Star Valley, then. It's big sky country. You can see all the stars you like.'

'It sounds wonderful.' He topped up their wineglasses. 'In a way it was star-gazing that led me into philosophy.'

'Really?'

'Yes. It was the summer after I left school and I was on a holiday with some mates, and we camped out on the beach at Byron Bay. It was the first time I'd really taken a good long look at the stars. You know, really looked at the sheer vastness and immensity of the universe.'

'It's a pretty awesome sight, isn't it?'

'It certainly is. It got me wondering how we humans fit into the scheme of things.'

'Does philosophy give answers to questions like that?'

'Not definitive answers necessarily, but it gives theories and possibilities. And it gives you guidance to work through all the existing answers till you work out your own.'

'And you've worked out yours?'

His eyes regarded her warmly. 'I'm getting there.'

Annie sighed. There was so much she wanted to ask Theo. Deep questions about the existence of God, about life and its possible meaning, but she didn't really know where to begin. 'So you went straight from school into philosophy?'

'No. My father wanted me to study something more practical, so I started out studying economics. I got into philosophy by accident.'

'How?'

He pulled a sheepish grin. 'You wouldn't be very impressed.'

'Try me.'

Hooking one arm over the back of his chair, he leaned back and sent her another self-conscious smile. 'I'm talking about centuries ago, remember, when I was eighteen and desperate to win on to girls, but terribly shy.'

Theo had been shy with girls? That was a surprise, but she refrained from saying so.

'I can't quite believe I'm telling you this, but at the time my older sister assured me that girls love brainy guys, so I hit on the idea of sitting in the backs of bars with a big fat book and a pipe and trying to look impressively clever.'

'A pipe, Theo?'

'It was unlit. I saw it as a symbol that linked me to all the great twentieth century thinkers.'

'And were the chicks impressed?'

'Actually, it was amazing how well it worked.'

I'll bet. Annie felt a surge of ridiculous jealousy for all the girls who'd scored a date with him. She took another deeper sip of her wine.

'Forgive me for being slow, but I don't quite get the connection between attracting girls and philosophy. Or do I have totally the wrong idea about philosophy?'

Theo laughed. 'One of the books I took along with me was about Seneca, a philosopher who lived in Roman times. I got so damned interested in him and his ideas that I forgot to keep an eye out for the girls. Apparently several tried to get my attention and gave up. From that night on I was hooked on philosophy.'

'And you gave up girls?' Annie feigned innocence.

'Well…no. Not exactly.'

Across their table their eyes met. Annie saw in Theo's gaze an unmistakable flash that sent shivers feathering her skin.

Taking a deep breath, she said, 'So what did this Roman guy have to say that impressed you so much?'

'Oh, many things.' He looked away again as he thought for a moment. 'Actually, you'd probably like him too, because you come from the outback.'

'There's a link between the outback and an ancient Roman philosopher?'

'You folk in the outback have adjusted your lives to cope with your environment. You accept that there are forces stronger than humans, forces that are completely indifferent to our desires. You've learned to endure bushfires and drought. Things that can't be changed. Seneca was big on accepting lessons from nature.'

Annie chuckled.

'What's so funny?'

'I wouldn't be too quick to congratulate us on accepting our lot in the bush, Theo. Why do you think I was cracking my neck to get to the city?'

He blinked.

'Heck, in the bush we get sick of making adjustments for *everything*—even something as simple as ordering books over the Internet.'

'That's a problem?'

'On most websites my postal address is invalid. They won't accept Southern Cross, via Mirrabrook. They tell me I need a street number and suburb or town. So I have to invent an address that keeps them happy.'

Theo smiled. 'And that's before you get to the big problems like droughts and floods.'

'Exactly.'

The next minute his expression grew sombre. And Annie knew she'd spoiled the mood. He'd remembered Damien and the email and how desperate she'd been to find a city boyfriend.

He cleared his throat. 'Anyhow… I'm afraid I can't spend more time chatting this evening. I have some pressing work that I must attend to tonight.'

She jumped to her feet. 'Of course. Let me clean up. You get on with what you have to do.'

· 'I'll need to show you where things go.'

In the kitchen they were terribly efficient. No more cosy chats as utensils and china were rinsed and the dishwasher was stacked.

Theo made coffee. As he offered Annie a cup he said, 'I'll take mine through to the study.'

'Okay.'

'Good night.'

''Night, Theo.' She watched him disappear, then thumbed through a current affairs magazine as she drank coffee in the empty kitchen with the humming dishwasher as her only companion.

Then she went back upstairs to Damien's bedroom, unzipped her bag and transferred her clothes into the wardrobe. Crumbs, it was empty. All Damien's clothes had been removed. How weird.

The room gave absolutely no hint of Damien's personality. Had that been deliberate? Sinking on to the edge of his bed, Annie looked around her and felt a faint stirring of unease. Surely it shouldn't have been necessary to remove everything from this room?

Then a sharper tingle of fear skittered down her spine as a horrible thought struck her. Perhaps Damien didn't exist!

No, that was silly. It would mean that Theo wasn't his uncle. Oh, God. Sudden panic sluiced through her. Could Theo *be* Damien? Was that why they both had the same tastes and ideas?

Could Theo have used Damien as an Internet code name and then hidden behind his real identity when she came to the city? Oh, God. The very thought made her head spin. Surely she was letting her imagination get the better of her. There had to be a more logical explanation.

But if there was it eluded her.

She'd moved in with a man she knew nothing about. For all she knew he could be leading two lives. That couldn't be very healthy.

A kind of fearful desolation descended on her as she prepared for bed. And she knew she was looking down the barrel of another sleepless night.

CHAPTER FIVE

MEL rang early the next afternoon.

'Just checking to see how everything's going,' she said, her voice purring suggestively.

'Fine,' Annie told her. 'I'm making risotto with smoked salmon and asparagus.'

'At this time of day?'

'Well, I'm starting from scratch. Making my own stock and everything.'

'Crumbs, Annie. I thought you'd be out, strolling around an art gallery, soaking up culture.'

'I did that this morning, but I wanted to—'

'Impress Dr Theo with your culinary skills?'

Yes. It was probably foolish of her to hope that she could impress Theo. A man had to be interested in her before he could be impressed, and Theo had been so remote this morning.

After her restless night she'd slept in and Theo hadn't woken her when he'd taken Basil for his walk. And he'd kept his nose in a newspaper while he had his breakfast coffee and toast. It was almost as an afterthought as he was heading out of the door that he'd mentioned he had theatre tickets for this evening and would she like to come.

But, foolish though it might be, she *wanted* to impress him with this meal.

Despite the mystery surrounding the whole Damien-Theo connection, she fancied the heck out of Theo and heaven knew, she was never going to impress him with her dazzling intellect.

'Theo's the most amazing cook, Mel. I can't just feed him sausages and mash.'

'Don't forget to have some fun, Annie. You told me you came down here to get out of the kitchen. I was going to ask if you wanted to do something tonight, but it sounds like you're busy.'

'Thanks for thinking of me. Theo said something about going to see a play.'

'Oh, nice.'

'I hope so. I haven't seen a stage play since our English teacher took us to see *A Midsummer Night's Dream*. Perhaps I can meet you for lunch tomorrow or the next day?'

'Okay. Keep in touch.' Mel sighed. 'I'm still not confident you're doing the right thing, Annie.'

'Relax, Mel. I'm totally on top of this,' Annie lied.

*   *   *

When the theatre lights came up at the end of the play, Theo discovered Annie dabbing at her eyes with a tissue.

'That was a terrible ending,' she said. 'I was expecting it to turn out happily.'

'So you insist on happy endings, do you?'

'Not necessarily, but when a play starts out like a romantic comedy I do. I was sure James and Erica would end up together, then in the last five minutes everything fell apart. That shouldn't be allowed. I was devastated.' She shoved the bunched tissue back into her purse and sniffed. 'Sorry.'

'No need to apologise.'

'I enjoyed every minute of it until the end.'

Annie looked so disappointed that Theo was tempted to throw a reassuring arm around her shoulders. He might have done so if she hadn't also been looking so lovely this evening.

Despite the hint of tears still shimmering in her eyes, she was radiant in her simple, sleeveless dark red dress. Slim and womanly. Breathtakingly so.

But he was determined to keep his distance, and as they joined the people filing out of the theatre he shoved his hands deep in the pockets of his trousers. He kept them there as he and Annie walked side by side back to his place, even though it was a perfect summery November's night.

A trip to the theatre had seemed a good idea, far safer than staying at home with Annie, being bewitched by the changing nuances in her animated face, or being flattered by her rapt attention during conversations; safer than waiting in pleasant anticipation of being ambushed by another of her unexpected questions, or thinking about an ambush or two of his own...that didn't involve quite so much talking...

And, as if that wasn't bad enough... Tonight the scent of frangipani lingered in the air and fallen jacaranda bells formed a carpet beneath their feet. A half moon rode at a tilt above the rooftops. It was the kind of night that cried out for a little romantic hand-holding, but he had to nip those kinds of thoughts in the bud.

Fat chance.

As they walked beneath trees and street lamps, passing in and out of shadows, he couldn't resist stealing glimpses in Annie's direction. She walked with an easy grace, a barely contained vitality. And whenever the light touched her hair it gleamed like a silken reflection of the pale gold moon. He longed to touch it.

Longed to feel the smooth curve of her

shoulders, the slenderness of her waist. And more.

He would be wiser to reserve his admiration for the brave tilt of her chin and the pert jut of her nose. But on a night like this wisdom crumbled so easily. *Damn!* He had always prided himself on his self-control and yet now he was thinking about Annie's legs. How was a man expected to remain immune to them? They were so devastatingly long and lovely beneath her red skirt.

To his dismay, he was forced to admit that he was losing the will to remain at a safe distance from Annie McKinnon. But he had to, damn it. There were a thousand reasons why getting close to her was unwise. Besides, she hadn't come to the city to meet *him*. She was far too young and spirited and lively to get involved with a boring university lecturer.

Annie felt strangely nervous by the time they reached Theo's house. There seemed to be a new tension between them, an almost tangible sexual tension. Or was she imagining that?

The mystery of Damien still loomed in the background of her thoughts, but she didn't know how to broach the subject without spoiling the mood of the evening. And tonight she didn't want to spoil anything. Every minute she spent with Theo convinced her that she was becoming helplessly attracted to him.

They entered his house by the front door and he paused in the middle of his lounge. 'Would you like coffee or brandy or both?'

'I think I'd like brandy but no coffee,' she said. 'Coffee tends to keep me awake.'

'Brandy it is, then. Take a seat.'

She sat in an armchair while he removed his coat and fetched glasses and brandy from a drinks cabinet. He handed her a glass and took a seat on the sofa, which was positioned at right angles to her chair.

Settling back, he loosened the knot of his tie and crossed an ankle over a knee. Then he slipped his glasses up on to his forehead while he massaged the bridge of his nose. He seemed relaxed, but Annie couldn't help wondering if, like her, he was making a conscious effort to look more relaxed than he felt.

His glasses back in place, he smiled at her and raised his drink. 'Cheers. Thanks for your company this evening.'

'Thank you for taking me, Theo. I really enjoyed the play, despite my fuss at the end.'

'Here's to happier endings.'

'I'll second that. Happy endings.'

Their gazes met and the sudden heat in

Theo's eyes was so electrifying that Annie was glad she was sitting down.

He took a deep sip of his drink. 'Thanks again for dinner, too. Your risotto was truly superb.'

'Glad you liked it.'

For a while they sat without talking, enjoying the fine brandy. But the prolonged quiet was too much for Annie.

'Theo, can I spoil this golden silence by asking another of my nosy questions?'

He smiled. 'Wait till I brace myself.' He drew an exaggerated deep breath. 'Okay. I suppose I'm as ready as I'll ever be. Fire when you're ready.'

'It's nothing too confronting. Well, perhaps it is a bit—it's just that ever since our conversation last night, I've been curious about your girlfriends.'

'Oh, dear.'

'Do you have a girlfriend at the moment?'

He didn't speak immediately. Keeping his gaze lowered, he said, 'I date women from time to time, but there's no one special at the moment.'

'Are you still shy with women?'

His face broke into a helpless grin and a knowing light sparked in his eyes. 'I don't hang around in bars with a book and a pipe, if that's what you're asking.'

The warmth of his amused gaze flowed over her and her cheeks felt hot. 'Fair enough. I'll let you off that particular hook for now.' Suddenly she kicked off her shoes and settled more comfortably into the armchair with her legs curled beneath her.

'That's the hard questions over. Now for the easy one.'

'I can hardly wait.'

'What do philosophers have to say about romance?'

His smile lurked, but he eyed her cautiously and he took a deep sip of brandy before he answered. 'On the whole, philosophers haven't been too impressed by romantic love. I think they feel it's best left to song writers and poets.'

'Why do they avoid it?'

'Well—romance interrupts more serious projects.'

She made a faintly scoffing sound.

'Even the greatest minds can become bewildered by the power of love.'

'Of course! So they should be.' Leaning over the arm of the chair, she challenged him. 'But surely you can't expect me to believe that all the philosophers, supposedly the greatest thinkers in the world, have put the entire subject of romantic love into the too hard basket?'

'Well, no, they haven't. Not entirely.'

'So?'

'You want examples? Okay, there was a German philosopher called Schopenhauer, who decided that love is perplexing and yet very important to us because the composition of the next generation depends on it.'

Annie stared at him in disbelief. 'Good grief, Theo. Was he serious?'

'Quite.'

'But that's the most unromantic, boring explanation anyone could ever think of. Is that the best philosophers can do?'

His smile was wry as he lifted his glass and watched the movement of the brandy as he gave it a little swirl. 'I admit that most fellows aren't really concerned about the continuation of the species when they ask a girl for her telephone number, but that's no reason to knock the idea.'

'Convince me.'

'The theory is that we are attracted to people whose genes will combine well with our own. For example, a man with a very big nose might be attracted to a woman with a rather small one and together they'll produce a child with a more acceptably sized nose.'

Annie tried hard not to stare at Theo's nose. She already knew that it was quite perfect, neither too big nor too small.

'But that's got next to nothing to do with romance,' she said. 'Not with the emotions and longings we feel deep in our hearts.'

He looked away for a moment and the muscles in his throat worked. 'We're speaking theoretically, Annie. And the theory is that this selection process works at a subconscious level. Apparently it explains why humans have an alarming propensity for falling in love with the wrong people.'

'Do they?'

'Yes. We've all seen it, haven't we? A man or a woman falls in love with someone who doesn't seem at all compatible, and yet they feel no sexual attraction whatsoever to someone who would be much more suitable.'

A sudden chill turned Annie's skin to goosebumps. 'Do you think that happens very often?'

'Of course. James and Erica in that play tonight were a very good example, but it happens all the time.'

She sat back and took another deeper sip of brandy. Staring down into her glass, she murmured, 'Perhaps that's why I'm so incredibly attracted to you.'

'I beg your pardon?'

Her heart pounded. 'I said perhaps that's why I'm so attracted to you.'

She looked up to find Theo staring at her. He looked predictably stunned, but at least he didn't look horrified.

'We're incompatible, aren't we? Take the education factor for starters.' She dropped her gaze back to her glass. 'Which is a pretty big factor.'

There was a stretch of silence. Then Theo said gently, 'I would have thought the gap in our ages was more of a problem.'

'It's not that big a gap. You could only be, what—ten years older than me?'

'Nine,' he amended quickly.

The speed of his answer and the scratchy sound in his voice, as if he'd swallowed a prickle, gave her courage. Leaning forward, she set her glass on the coffee table. 'Well, there you go, Theo. The incompatibilities are toppling by the minute.'

'Yes.' Without taking his eyes from hers, he set his glass down beside her glass. 'Perhaps they are.'

There was a moment of breathless stillness and silence while they both sat, watching each other, aware that they hovered on the brink of something momentous.

Then, to her dismay, Theo closed his eyes and released a soft groan. 'Annie, your honesty is refreshing but we shouldn't be talking like this.'

'Why not?'

'We need to step back from this for a moment and think.'

'Do we?' Annie winced when she heard the disappointment in her voice. She sighed and repositioned herself, uncurling her legs and sitting straight in the armchair once more. 'What do you suggest we think about?'

'Why you came to the city. What you really want. I assume you were hoping for adventure and romance, but you expected to find it with another younger person. And now I've intruded into the scene.'

She suspected that this was the moment to bring up her worries about Damien. Problem was, whenever she was with Theo, her whacko theories that he was leading a double life just didn't make any kind of sense. He was too grounded, too balanced, for subterfuge. And why would a man as gorgeous as Theo need to hunt for a woman using the Internet?

'To be honest, I'm not too interested in Damien any more,' she said.

'Nevertheless you should be out on the

town—hitting the top night spots with your girlfriends. Meeting younger men.'

'I enjoy being with you.'

He sighed. 'I'm not the kind of man you want to get involved with.'

'Why?' Nerves tightened in her stomach. Was this confession time? 'What's wrong with you?'

'I'm an excessively boring academic.'

'Boring?' She gaped at him. 'Is that all?'

He frowned. 'Were you expecting me to offer you a list of character faults?'

'No, no, not a list exactly.'

'You've already dismissed my claim that I'm too old for you, although I think that deserves closer consideration.'

'It's just that I thought you were going to bring some surprise skeleton out of the closet.'

He favoured her with a small smile and shook his head, and she felt a heady rush of relief.

'No skeletons,' he said. 'But perhaps you think that in itself is boring?'

'Theo, in no way are you boring. Honestly, from where I'm looking, you're shaping up to be the single most interesting man I've ever met.'

A dark colour stained his cheekbones. His eyes flashed with sudden heat. For a breathless moment Annie thought he was going to leap out of his chair and haul her on to the sofa with him.

If only...

Clenching a fist on his knee, he looked away, and she saw his jaw tighten with tension.

After a clamouring stretch of silence he said, 'What surprises me is that a lovely girl like you had to come to Brisbane to search for a boyfriend. I would have thought you'd have plenty of offers, even though you're relatively isolated in the outback.'

For a moment she couldn't answer. She was too busy indulging in a private celebration because Theo had said she was lovely. *Wow!* With an effort, she forced her mind to process the rest of his comment.

'I've tried dating guys from the bush,' she said, 'but after a while I lost interest in them. I suppose I fit right in with that German philosopher's theory. It would have been sensible of me to fall for a man in the outback, but no one clicked. I don't know why. Maybe it's because I've had a steady diet of cowboys all my life that I find city men much more interesting.'

Theo's response was to sit very still and scowl at a spot on the floor, which made Annie feel suddenly flooded by doubts. And very foolish. And exposed.

Had she completely misinterpreted their situation? She'd thought there was a mutual 'something' happening between them, but perhaps she'd got it all wrong. Maybe Theo was trying to suggest kindly, indirectly, that he was regretting his offer of hospitality?

A horrible flash of chilling panic slithered through her. She bent down and picked up her shoes, then stood. No doubt it was an immature, reckless, *un*-philosophical way to respond, but she couldn't help herself. 'I can move back to Mel's in the morning, if that's what you want.'

Then, because she suddenly felt the need to cry, she turned and hurried across the room without waiting for his reply.

'Goodnight,' she called over her shoulder before scooting up the stairs.

Theo watched her go.

Common sense and logic told him it was best for Annie to return to her girlfriends in the morning. He'd invited her to his house on an impulsive, foolish whim, fuelled by more self-interest than he'd cared to admit at the time, but it was not too late to correct his mistake.

In a flash of images, he pictured himself doing the right thing—driving her back to her friends and then returning to this house without her. Saw himself walking with Basil along the South Bank. Morning after morning. Without her. Saw himself dating sensible academic colleagues—taking them to see plays—women who would never dissolve into tears over the ending, however unsatisfactory.

And the thought appalled him so fiercely that he jumped to his feet, charged across the room and took the stairs three at a time.

Annie was in the doorway of Damien's room—about to close the door.

'I don't want you to go, Annie,' he said.

With her hand on the doorknob, she turned back to him, her face pale and her eyes shining with a suspicious brightness. 'No?'

He shook his head and smiled. 'In fact, I'd very much like you to stay.'

She lifted the shoes she'd been holding and cradled them against her chest in a kind of defensive gesture. 'Why have you changed your mind?'

'One very good reason.' He smiled. 'Honestly, from where I'm looking, you're shaping up to be the single most interesting woman I've ever met.'

For a moment she looked confused. Her

clear blue eyes reflected disbelief warring with wonder. But then a slow, warm smile suffused her face. 'That's nice to know,' she said.

But instead of running into his arms with the open-hearted impulsiveness he'd come to expect from her, she said a demure goodnight and closed her bedroom door.

And yet again, Dr Theo Grainger was left with a feeling of puzzled inadequacy.

CHAPTER SIX

Yes! Yes! Yes!

Annie danced in happy circles, waving her shoes above her head. Theo found her interesting. Not just any old interesting, but terribly interesting—the *most* interesting woman ever. And he'd also said she was lovely.

She waltzed around Damien's room. *Lovely.* Wasn't that the most scrumptious word in the whole dictionary?

Spinning another ecstatic circle, she knew that Theo was lovely too. Exceptionally lovely. In a completely masculine way, of course. She loved everything about him, from the topmost hair on his head to—

A curt knock sounded on her door.

In the middle of executing a wicked pirouette, she wobbled precariously. Then promptly lost her balance. Her shoes flew from her hands as she tumbled to the floor at the precise moment the door opened.

Theo.

From an undignified heap at his feet, and

with her dress riding high up her thighs, she looked up at him and blushed.

'I'm so sorry,' he said, bending to offer her a helping hand. 'I didn't mean to startle you.'

There was little she could do except take the hand he offered and allow herself to be helped to her feet.

'Are you hurt?'

'No, not at all.' Blushing again, she smoothed her dress over her hips and thighs, and took a calming deep breath before lifting her eyes to meet his. 'Did you—um—want something, Theo?'

'Yes.' Amusement danced in his hazel eyes. 'I wanted to double-check something you said earlier. I have an urgent need to be quite clear about it.'

She stared at him blankly for a moment. She'd said so many things this evening. 'Which something would that be?'

His smile was the sexy kind that turned her insides to marshmallow.

'Was it my imagination, or did you say something about being attracted to me?'

'Oh.' Heat suffused her. 'Well, yes, I did, because it's true. I *am* attracted to you, Theo.'

Taking her hands in his, he smiled again. 'Good. Because, in case you haven't guessed, the attraction's mutual.'

'It is?'

'Very.'

For a heartbeat they smiled into each other's eyes, and then Theo drew Annie gently towards him, and it was as easy as spring slipping into summer, the way she melted into his arms.

His lips brushed her cheek. 'I'm very, very attracted.'

'Same here. Think of me as a dropped pin and you're a magnet.'

His chuckle caressed her skin. 'There's no way I'm going to think of you as a dropped pin.'

Her eyes drifted closed as his lips explored her jawline. 'I suppose it does sound dangerous.'

He pressed a kiss to the corner of her mouth. 'You *are* dangerous, Annie McKinnon.'

'No, I'm—'

He stopped her protest with a kiss on the lips.

Oh, man!

Oh, bliss, to be kissed by Theo. Bliss to be enclosed within the strong circle of his arms and to feel his lovely lips tracing dreamy patterns on hers. Joy to let her lips drift open as his kiss turned hot and brandy-flavoured. Heaven as his mouth seduced her.

She pressed closer, wriggling her hips against his hard, masculine body. And Theo's gentlemanly reserve became a thing of the past.

His mouth became demanding. His tongue delved deep while his hands moulded her shoulders, then the shape of her breasts through her dress. Soft groans rumbled low in his throat as he began to walk her slowly backwards to Damien's bed.

Damien!

Oh, help!

A wretched alarm bell pierced Annie's consciousness.

The thought of Damien pulled her up sharply, like a rough hand dragging her back from the point of drowning.

Damn, Damien. The spectre of him was beside them, like a ghostly presence in this strangely bare room...

Darn. Why did she have to think of the jerk now? Why did her worries about the Theo-Damien connection have to surface at this crucial point in time—possibly the most decisive moment in her lifetime?

Theo, sensing her sudden tension, grew still. 'Is something the matter?'

She didn't want to speak, didn't want to

spoil this delicious, all-important moment, but the word spilled out. 'Damien.'

'Damien?'

She could hear the raggedness of his breathing. His eyes met hers and for long seconds he stared at her, looking puzzled and worried, before he released her and took a step back.

'You're still infatuated with Damien?'

'No, of course not.' She felt so overcome she had to cover her face with her hands.

'What is it, Annie? Have I frightened you?'

'No, no, Theo.' She dropped her hands to her sides again, then looked around her. 'It's just this room—I just don't understand who Damien is, where he's gone, or why he pretended to be you, or why you've stripped his room bare. It's kind of getting to me. It makes me nervous. Half the time I'm afraid that—that—'

'What? What are you afraid of?'

She was almost too afraid to say it. 'That he's you.'

'*Me?*'

Theo looked so clearly appalled that Annie felt instant relief.

'I've been plagued by this horrible thought that Damien might have been your Internet persona. You know, like a code name.'

'Oh, Annie.' Theo shook his head and raked a hand through his thick dark hair. Staring at the floor, he let out a huff of irritation. 'It's time that wretched nephew of mine faced up to the consequences of his own foolishness.'

Annie gulped. 'I'm so sorry, Theo. I didn't mean to blab it out now. I didn't want to spoil things.'

'No, you're right,' he said. 'It's better to clear the air. I'm going to get on to Damien right away and insist he comes back to apologise to you.'

His eyes shimmered darkly with emotion as he reached out and traced his fingers down the curve of her cheek. His mouth quirked into a lopsided smile. 'It was probably best that you spoke up when you did. Someone needed to apply the brakes.'

Her hand closed over his as it lay against her cheek. Turning her face, she kissed the inner curve of his palm.

His breath escaped on a soft sigh. Bending closer, he pressed a warm kiss to the back of her neck. 'I'll say goodnight, Annie, before I'm tempted to go back on my word. Hopefully, you'll have your answer about Damien tomorrow.'

He left her room quickly and she turned back to look around Damien's bedroom, awash with a tumble of emotions—with relief, with happiness, but also with regret and longing.

But, with the imprint of Theo's lovely kisses lingering warmly on her lips, she knew she would sleep well tonight.

Next morning, after a pre-breakfast run with Theo and Basil, Annie was in the shower when she heard a young man's voice penetrate the hiss of water streaming over her.

'What the hell's going on? Where are my things?'

She paused in the process of rinsing shampoo from her hair. Was there someone in her room?

'Where's my stereo and my CD collection?' the voice shouted again. It was louder. Angrier. 'And where's my DVD player? What have you done to my flaming room?'

Snapping off the taps, she stood, naked and dripping.

Fists hammered on the bathroom door. 'Who's in there?'

'Hold your horses!' she yelled back, scrambling out of the shower cubicle so quickly she stubbed her toe.

In panicky haste she snatched a towel and wrapped it around her. Her wet feet threatened to slip on the tiled bathroom floor as she hurried to the rattling door. With one hand clutching the towel tightly over her chest, she opened the door six inches.

And blinked.

A gangling, bespectacled boy stood there—an angry looking boy in his late teens, wearing a T-shirt and Hawaiian print board shorts. And sandals.

At the sight of her his jaw dropped so fast he risked dislocation. His eyes practically popped out of his head.

Annie was just as shocked. 'Who—w-what—?'

She was rescued from her stammering question by Theo charging through the bedroom doorway like a cattle truck out of control.

'Get out of this room immediately,' he roared at the boy.

'Hey, steady on, Theo. You can't order me back from the Gold Coast and then tell me to get out of my own bedroom.'

'You've abdicated all rights to this room for the foreseeable future.'

Stunned, Annie stared at them both.

This couldn't be Damien. Not this boy. For heaven's sake, he couldn't be more than seventeen or eighteen. He still had spots on his chin. Where was the surfer streaked hair from the photo he'd sent her? The movie-star-sexy good looks?

The intruder switched his attention from Theo to her and his face turned beetroot. 'Oh, God. It's Annie, isn't it?'

Her last lingering hope sank without a trace. No chance for error now. This was Damien. *This was her Dream Date!*

Sick to the stomach, she sagged against the doorjamb. Then, as Damien continued to stare at her, she remembered with a jolt of embarrassment that a bath towel was not appropriate clothing for this encounter.

Theo, who was similarly damp but at least dressed, must have realised the same thing. Grabbing Damien by the neck of his T-shirt, he hauled him out of the room.

'But how was I to know?' the boy shouted. 'You sent me a text message ordering me back home and here I am. How did Annie get here? What's going on?'

She could hear Damien's continued protests and Theo's raised voice as he dragged the boy downstairs.

Good grief! Closing the bathroom door, she leaned against it and her stomach churned. Damien—a kid *barely out of school*. She felt such a fool as she thought of all the weeks she'd blissfully exchanged emails with him.

For crying out loud, she'd flirted with him. Shamelessly. In her typical, take-no-prisoners fashion, she'd spilled out her heart and soul in those emails. She'd even discussed her feelings for him with the agony aunt in the *Mirrabrook Star*.

How humiliating! All that excitement she'd felt had been over a date with a skinny kid still clawing his way out of puberty.

Her mind cringed. But then, hot on the heels of her embarrassment, came a burst of anger. The nerve of him to deceive her, to play games with her like that! What a grub!

She remembered all the names Mel and Victoria had used to describe him after the disastrous non-date. He deserved every one of them.

Peeling the towel away from her, she wrenched the bathroom door open again, hurried into the bedroom and dragged on jeans and a T-shirt. No way was she going to hide away in the bathroom feeling humiliated when she could give the little twerp a piece of her mind.

Without a care for her messy wet hair, she hurried downstairs.

Theo and Damien were glaring at each other across the kitchen.

'I don't care where you go,' Theo growled.

'You're not welcome here. Once you've apologised to Annie, you can go back to your mates at the Gold Coast.'

'So I'm being thrown out because Annie McKinnon's moved in?'

An embarrassed grimace flickered over Theo's face, but he covered it with fresh anger. 'It's time you accepted the consequences of your actions, Damien. You've caused Miss McKinnon inconvenience and expense and embarrassment. It's time to grow up. You're legally an adult, but no one would know it from the way you behave.'

Realising that Annie was in the room, Damien turned her way and he reddened again when he saw her. 'I'm sorry, Annie.'

'So you jolly well should be,' she said sternly.

'And how about a proper apology?' added Theo.

Damien scowled at him. 'What do you mean?'

'You can do better than merely mumbling you're sorry. I want you to stand here in front of Miss McKinnon and look her in the eye and tell her exactly what you're apologising for.'

'There's no need to jump down my throat. She knows why I'm sorry.'

Theo's fists clenched as if Damien had

tested his patience once too often. 'Tell her, or you'll get a good clip on the ear.'

Annie didn't believe Theo would carry out his threat. Nevertheless, tension quivered in the air as Damien glowered back at his uncle and his own fists curled in response. But the nephew knew he was in the wrong and his defiance wilted.

He dropped his gaze to the floor. 'I apologise—' he began.

'Speak to Annie,' ordered Theo. 'Look at her.'

Another flash of resentment flared, but then Damien took a deep breath, squared his shoulders and turned to Annie. 'I really am sorry, Annie.' His Adam's apple slid up and down in his youthful throat. 'I guess I shouldn't have gone to a dating chat room in the first place, and when you told me how old you were, I shouldn't have strung you along. It all started out as a bit of fun and it went too far. I—I'm sorry about the d—date and everything. I didn't really think you'd show up.'

Her eyes narrowed. 'It's not very pleasant to discover I've been used, Damien. I value myself more highly than a form of amusement for a youngster with raging hormones.'

He flushed more brightly.

'You don't look much like your photo,' she

added and he looked so hugely embarrassed that she began to feel sorry for him.

Theo chipped in. 'And I didn't appreciate the way you dashed off leaving some garbled message and expecting me to pick up the pieces. So I've told Annie that she's welcome to use your room for as long as she wants to stay in Brisbane.'

About to protest, Damien thought better of it. 'So where's all my gear?'

'It's been stored at Pop's.'

He seemed relieved to hear that and he nodded slowly. 'Maybe Pop will take pity on me and let me stay at his place.'

'You don't deserve any kind of pity,' said Theo. 'But no doubt your grandfather will relent. It'll be up to you to explain to him why you don't have a roof over your head.'

'No roof?' Annie felt suddenly guilty.

Theo shot her a quick warning frown. 'Don't worry about him. My father will take him in.'

Apparently resigned to his fate now, Damien slung a small blue backpack over his shoulder. Annie couldn't help noticing the family resemblance between the youth and the uncle. It wasn't just that they both had steady hazel eyes, or the fact that they were both tall and had the same shiny dark hair—or that they both wore glasses.

With his confession behind him, Damien's face showed the beginnings of the same intelligence and strength of character she'd found so readily in Theo's. In another six or seven years, when Damien filled out and matured, the resemblance would be even stronger.

Now, he backed towards the door. 'I hope you enjoy my room, Annie.' He spoke with a polite dignity that was another echo of his uncle. But then the effect was spoiled by a cheeky smirk. 'But it can't be much fun for you hanging around here with old Uncle Theo.'

'Get going,' barked Theo.

Damien went.

'Oh, boy.' Annie felt shaken and she sank on to a kitchen stool.

Theo was watching her, his eyes shadowed with concern. 'I'm sorry you had to find out about him so abruptly.'

She frowned. 'Why did you keep him a secret? Couldn't you have told me sooner?'

He began to fill the coffee maker. 'I was trying to spare you.'

'From embarrassment?' She managed a wan smile. 'So you cleared all his things out of his room because you didn't want me to realise how young he was?'

'Yes.'

She nodded, then sighed. 'Actually, that was kind of you. I must admit I feel pretty small when I think how gullible I was to come charging down here for a big city date—with a *teenager*.'

She stared at the dazzle of morning sunlight streaming through the glass doors from the courtyard, thinking of that happy, excited self who'd come rushing to the city, full of high hopes.

'I was so worked up about coming away for that date I actually asked for advice from a columnist in the *Mirrabrook Star*.'

'What's that?'

She rolled her eyes. 'Our little local newspaper.'

Theo smiled. 'Were you given good advice?'

'Yes, it was excellent. It was exactly what I wanted to hear.' Annie's answering smile was cheeky as she rose and walked across the room and stood in the sun's warmth, fluffing her damp hair with her hands to help it to dry.

Behind her, the room began to fill with the delicious aroma of coffee and she began to feel calmer. After all, anger was a choice, and why spoil a beautiful morning when the mystery of the Damien-Theo link had finally been laid to rest.

'How did Damien come to live with you?' she asked. 'Are you his guardian?'

'No, he's my sister's boy, but she's a single mother and when Damien hit his teens he became too much for her to handle. As I'm sure you can imagine from this latest stunt!'

'You took over raising him?'

'Jane felt he was lacking in male guidance and I volunteered to lend a hand. It ended up becoming more or less a permanent arrangement.'

She stared at him as she digested this. 'So you've looked after Damien all though his high school years?'

'That's right.'

'Solo?'

He nodded.

'It can't have been easy for you.'

Theo shrugged. 'I'll admit he's been a challenge. But Jane was working flat out to make a go of her career and she and Damien were having terrible clashes.'

He reached into an overhead cupboard for coffee cups. 'I must admit there have been occasions when he's almost been too much for me. But, on the whole, he's not a bad kid—

just *young*. Half his problem is he's too damn smart.'

'Is he a university student?'

'Not yet. He decided to take a year off between school and university. And I supported that decision. I thought it was a good idea to let him mature a bit before he started studying. He's been working as a waiter in a bar, but it's not enough to keep him occupied. And, as you said, his hormones are rampant. Spare time and eighteen-year-old hormones are not a good combination.'

'Maybe he'll settle down next year when he gets his teeth into some serious study.'

'Yes, I'm quietly confident that he'll turn out okay.'

Annie nodded. 'I don't doubt that Damien's very clever. He certainly has a way with words. I got no hint from his emails that he was a teenager.' She shot Theo a shy smile. 'He obviously holds you in very high regard.'

'What makes you say that?'

'When he was writing to me he modelled himself on you.'

'By claiming to love Italy and philosophy?'

'And Basil. He was very entertaining, very interesting. Sweet and charming, too.'

A wave of heat swept over her as she remembered the way she'd described him in the

Ask Auntie letter. 'I thought he was a wonderfully warm, funny and clever man.' She shot him a coy smile. 'A man like you.'

Across the kitchen their eyes met and Annie felt a sweet pang of longing, that tug of attraction that snatched at her breath.

She distracted herself by hurrying to help with breakfast—dropping slices of bread into the toaster and fetching plates from the cupboard. And she was relieved when the toast popped up and she could busy herself buttering it while Theo poured their coffees.

But as they carried their mugs and plates out to the little table in the courtyard, she laughed suddenly.

'What's the joke?' he asked.

'I just saw the funny side of this.'

'Which is?'

'Damien's efforts on the Internet aren't all that different from the antics of a certain young man, who shall remain nameless, who used to try to attract girls by sitting in the backs of bars with a scholarly book and a pipe.'

Theo's valiant attempt to look angry failed. 'You'll keep, Annie McKinnon,' he said as a reluctant smile twitched his lips. 'You'll keep.'

* * *

'Theo's invited me to some sort of staff social function at the university,' Annie told Mel when she phoned her mid-morning.

'Far out, Annie! Do you really have to go?'

'I guess so,' she said, feeling a little taken aback by Mel's reaction. 'I told Theo I'd go, but I must say I'm a bit nervous. I've been trying to swot up on philosophy this morning and I've been thumbing through some of his books, but not much is sticking. Do you have any tips?'

'Heck, no. I've forgotten most of the philosophy I ever learned.'

'The ideas are so hard to hang on to. I get to the point where I think I've got my head around a concept, but the minute I try to move on to the next idea, the first one slides straight out of my head. I feel so dumb.'

Mel chuckled. 'Believe me, you're not dumb, Annie. Why do you think people spend years studying philosophy in incremental stages, rather than trying to cram centuries of accumulated wisdom into a half an hour?'

'I guess.' Annie sighed. 'Do you think philosophers talk about the weather and the quality of the wine like ordinary people?'

'For Pete's sake, they *are* ordinary people. But, whatever you do, don't let them know you've figured that out.' There was a pause and then Mel said, 'Annie, you're going all out to impress this guy, aren't you?'

'He's worth it, Mel.' Annie closed her eyes. She tingled all over whenever she thought about tonight—especially when she thought about coming home from this function—and taking up where she and Theo had left off last night—exploring their mutual attraction.

'If you want my advice,' said Mel, 'take a nice long bubble bath and shampoo your hair and paint your toenails. Forget the cramming. Just wear a short skirt and those professors won't be grilling you to find out what you know about Socrates.'

'Mel, you used to be such a feminist. What happened?'

'I slammed up against real life. Hey, I've got to go, Annie. The boss is looking daggers. Catch you tomorrow.'

'Okay.'

'And try to have fun tonight.'

'I'll do my best.'

The minute Annie and Theo arrived at the faculty cocktail party, she realised that enjoying herself was going to be a bigger challenge than she'd feared. For starters, she'd made a terrible mistake. Her dress was totally wrong.

She should have paid attention this morning

when Theo assured her that the dark red dress she'd worn to the play last night would be fine for this evening's function. She certainly shouldn't have gone back to the shop where she'd bought the pink jeans and she most definitely should not have gone anywhere near the racks of glittery party wear that Victoria had warned her against.

But they'd been calling to her.

And she'd fallen head over heels in love with the most divine little dress, covered with tawny pink pearls and softly shimmering sequins.

When she'd tried it on she'd been blown away by the transformation. It was as if she'd been touched by a magic wand and turned into a film star. She loved it. From the fine spaghetti straps to the scalloped knee-length hem, the dress was gorgeous. It clung softly to her shape, but was tastefully demure and its understated colour toned fabulously with her complexion.

But it was fabulously wrong.

She realised that now as she stood, frozen in horror, in the doorway of the university's Staff and Graduates Club. Her spirits sank through the soles of her sequinned sandals.

She turned to Theo. 'Why didn't you warn me?'

'What about?'

'My dress. It's all wrong.'

'It isn't, Annie. It's wonderful.'

'But everyone else is in black.'

'Not everyone.'

Her eyes skirted the room. 'Just about.'

In the far corner, surrounded by a little forest of potted palms, earnest, black-clad musicians were playing a string quartet. Everywhere else, people with drinks in their hands were standing and talking quietly in dignified groups.

The men were wearing dinner suits, but apart from a very arty looking woman draped in an exotic profusion of scarves, the women were wearing elegant, conservative dresses in subdued hues like black, dark smoky-blue or deep claret. Even brown.

Nothing pink—tawny or otherwise. And certainly nothing sparkly. Unless you counted the occasional head of silver hair.

If only she could run away and hide.

These people belonged together. They were an exclusive club. And for Annie they spelled *other*. Not her crowd.

But Theo placed a protective hand at the small of her back and ushered her forward.

And a woman who looked a well-preserved, supremely confident, sixty years of age, hurried towards them. 'Theo, dear, I'm so pleased you could come.' She had one of those deep, mellifluous, cultured voices that made Annie instantly nervous. She smiled at Annie. 'How do you do, my dear? I'm Harriet Fletcher.'

'Hello, Harriet.' At least Annie's hand wasn't trembling visibly as she held it out.

Shaking hands, Harriet said, 'You haven't been to one of these evenings before, have you?'

'No.'

To Annie's surprise, Harriet took her arm as if they'd been friends for years. 'Then let me prise you away from Theo so you can meet everyone. Theo, you can look after Annie's drink.'

'Champagne?' he called to her as she was led away.

'Yes, please.'

Before she knew it, Annie had a glass of champagne in her hand and, under Harriet Fletcher's supervision, had been introduced to a dizzying whirlwind of strangers. But, too soon, more new guests arrived and Harriet hurried away to greet them. Annie looked around for Theo, but couldn't catch sight of him, which meant she was left alone with a group of people whose names she couldn't remember.

Shoulders back, Annie.

She turned to her right and discovered a bearded, balding fellow with a pleasant face. When she smiled and said hello, he patiently reintroduced himself and she responded warmly.

'Are you staff?' he asked.

'No. I'm a guest of Theo Grainger.'

He nodded. 'And what's your field?'

'My field?' For a frantic moment her mind flew into a panic. In desperation, she tried to jest. 'Would a paddock of Brahman steers count?'

This was met by a look of utter bewilderment.

'I'm sorry, that was a very bad joke. I don't have a field of study. Not yet, at any rate. You see, I help my brothers to run a cattle property in North Queensland.'

'How fascinating,' he said, returning her smile.

And, to her surprise, she realised he meant it. He really was interested. He told her that he was an environmental scientist and that he'd conducted studies on the river systems in North Queensland.

By the time Theo found her, she and the scientist were deep in a discussion of the varieties of fish that inhabited the Star River.

They chatted for another five minutes or so and then Theo said, 'I'm afraid I must drag Annie away to meet some members of the philosophy staff.'

And Annie's nervousness returned. These people would be Theo's particular friends. What would they think of her? Her stomach clenched as she crossed the room beside him.

'Are they all terribly clever?' she asked.

He smiled. 'Terribly.'

Oh, crumbs. She couldn't remember a thing she'd read in his philosophy books this morning.

Halfway across the room, she gripped his hand. 'I'm scared,' she said.

He stopped and looked down at her. 'You can't be, Annie. You're fearless.'

'What makes you think that?'

'I saw how brave you were when—' He suddenly shut his mouth as if he'd had second thoughts.

'When?'

Instead of answering, he lifted her hand to his lips and he kissed her fingers. Right there in front of everyone. And his tender smile was so beautiful she felt she might burst into tears.

'Just be yourself, Annie,' he said. 'These people will love you. Come on.'

They'd been heading for a group in the corner and now several faces, both friendly and curious, watched their approach. Annie couldn't help noticing that none of the men in the group had beards or looked remotely like scruffy absent-minded professors. Nor, for that matter, did the women.

Introductions were made and the atmosphere was relaxed and friendly as Theo explained that Annie was on a short visit from North Queensland.

'How did you stumble across our Theo?' asked a tall, dark, rather elegant woman, who'd been introduced simply as Claudia.

Annie hadn't been prepared for that question and her mouth turned dry as desert dust, but Theo rescued her.

'Through my young nephew, Damien,' he said. 'The two of them met chatting about philosophy over the Internet.'

'So you're a fellow philosopher?' someone else asked.

Somehow, Annie managed to unglue her tongue from the roof of her mouth. 'Oh, no,' she said. 'I'm interested—fascinated, actually. But my understanding is very superficial. I think it might take me a thousand years to come to grips with Aristotle alone.'

This was met by sympathetic smiles.

'What's young Damien doing these days?' a man called Rex asked Theo.

'All the wrong things,' Theo growled.

'How old is he now? About eighteen?'

Theo nodded.

'Six months working on a cattle property as a jackaroo would do him good,' Annie suggested, and behind her back she crossed her fingers, hoping that she hadn't been too outspoken.

To her relief, her comment was met with unanimous agreement.

'I read about a young eighteen-year-old who spent three months droving two thousand head of cattle across Queensland on his own,' Rex said.

'That's pretty amazing,' said Theo.

A middle-aged man shook his head. 'My kids could never cope with that kind of challenge. Apart from anything else, they couldn't go anywhere without their Discmans.'

'Or home-delivered pizzas,' added a woman who was probably his wife.

A plate of smoked oysters was passed around.

'That colour suits you wonderfully, Annie,' a woman in the group commented.

'Actually, I've been wondering what you'd

call a colour like that,' said Claudia, less kindly.

There was something about Claudia that unsettled Annie. Now, recognising that a deliberate shot had been fired, she couldn't resist firing back. 'The girl in the shop called it naked shimmer.'

Rex chuckled. 'Naked shimmer. I like that. Whatever it's called, it should be compulsory.'

Claudia rolled her eyes and pulled her mouth into a tightly contemptuous pout.

And Annie prayed that the conversation would steer on to something else. Surely these people had deeper, more serious things to talk about? But it seemed that Claudia didn't want to let her off the hook.

'How are you coping with life in the city?' Her smile was faintly patronising.

'I think I'm coping just fine, thank you. I love it here.'

'Don't you miss the wholesomeness of the country—those wide open spaces and all that fresh air?'

'I can't say that I do.' Annie smiled pleasantly. 'I miss my dog, but Theo's Dalmatian, Basil, makes up for her.'

Claudia's right eyebrow hiked high. 'Basil's a darling, isn't he?'

Despite the warm words, there was a new

brittle edge in Claudia's voice. She shot a swift glance towards Theo and a disturbing watchfulness dimmed her dark eyes. And Annie realised with a prickle of alarm that this woman had almost certainly been involved with Theo at some time in the past. Had they been lovers?

And swiftly following that thought came another. It was quite, *quite* possible that Theo's gesture of kissing her hand in full view of everyone had been more significant than she'd realised.

CHAPTER SEVEN

THEO doubted he could take much more of sharing Annie with a crowd. His colleagues were finding her as intriguing as he did. But ever since last night when he'd kissed her the sole focus of his thoughts had been kissing her again.

Tonight, in her fascinating skin-toned dress, she was driving him wild with the need to touch her, to hold her and taste her.

At last the buzz of conversation was interrupted by Professor Gilmore clearing his throat into a microphone, and everyone's attention turned to the little dais near the musicians where a microphone had been set up. Taking Annie's hand, he drew her away from the crowd, towards the back of the room.

'This is the formal part of the evening. Speeches and presentations,' he told her. 'So from now on the night gets even more boring.'

'But I haven't been bored. Your friends are very nice.' *Correction, most of them are nice.*

'You've been a big hit,' he murmured. 'But let's get out of here.'

She turned to him, her blue eyes round with surprise. 'Already?'

He hoped his smile didn't look wolfish. 'Yes, we've done our duty. There's no need to hang around. Come on, let's go while no one's looking.'

Still holding her hand, he led the way out through a side door.

'Where are we going?' she asked.

'Home.'

'Oh.' A pink tide rose from her neck to her face.

'Is that okay with you, Annie?'

'Yes,' she said quickly. 'Yes, of course.'

As they walked through the university grounds to the car park, it took every ounce of Theo's restraint to stop himself from hauling her into one of the dark recesses along the way and pressing her against a wall while he kissed her senseless. What the hell had come over him? It was years and years since he'd felt so out of control.

And yet, he'd never needed control more.

Annie might be enthusiastic and uninhibited, but there was an air of trusting innocence about her too. She was young. She was vulnerable.

He had no idea how experienced she was with men. She needed to be wooed. She deserved gentle loving.

Over the past twenty-four hours he'd thought it through a thousand times in his imagination. And he burned with his plans for making love to her—slowly, with exquisite restraint and sensitivity.

At least, that was the plan.

Annie could hardly breathe. Her sense of anticipation was excruciating.

Although nothing had been said, she knew deep in her bones why Theo was leaving the function early. Their physical awareness of each other had been building ever since last night and now they were both so turned on the atmosphere between them was almost crackling with electricity.

When they reached Theo's car he opened the door for her. She was too self-conscious to look at him. She slipped quickly into the passenger seat and when her bare shoulder brushed against his coat sleeve a flame of heat shot through her.

The heat burned inside her while she listened to his footsteps crunching on gravel as he walked around the back of the car. Her chest grew tight as he opened his door and lowered his long body into the driver's seat beside her. Tonight he'd pulled the car's hood in place so she wouldn't be blown about, and the tang of his aftershave reached her in the confined space.

Without speaking, he turned the key in the ignition, revved the motor and his sports car took off, zooming through the night like a low-flying jet. *Omigosh.* Annie had to remind herself to breathe.

Theo was taking her home...to make love to her.

She was acutely aware of every inch of his body so close beside her. She watched his hands resting lightly on the steering wheel, watched the purposeful movements of his left hand as he shifted the gear stick. He had very nice hands—strong, confident, capable. Perfect.

Crumbs, I'm forgetting to breathe again.

She leaned back against the cool leather of the car seat and closed her eyes. But that was no good because it encouraged her to imagine Theo's hands touching her. Another burst of heat flared inside her.

Eyes open again, she tried to concentrate on the city-scape that flashed past them. In a kind of daze she watched flickering neon signs and the traffic lights changing from red to green, the yellow rectangles of windows in office blocks. She looked at the traffic, which seemed to be engaged in a wickedly daring dance of ducking and weaving between lanes. After the bumpy and unlit outback tracks she was used to, everything in the city was so exciting and dangerous.

Closer to the city centre the buildings grew taller. No chance to see the moon or the stars. But it didn't matter. Tonight, everything she wanted was right beside her, driving expertly, hurrying home.

If only she wasn't feeling so nervous. Why couldn't she be cool about this? *Come off it, Annie. No girl could be cool about sex with Dr Theo Grainger.* This was a Big Deal! No doubt about it.

Would Theo be able to tell how long it was since she'd made love? Was he used to experienced, sophisticated lovers? Women like Claudia?

His voice broke the silence. 'I half-expected you to bombard me with questions all the way home.'

'I'm—um—I'm fresh out of questions.'

For once, she couldn't think of *anything* to say. And neither, it seemed, could Theo. He drove on in silence till they reached his house and he parked the car in the garage. They both made a fuss of Basil, who was prancing about their legs with his tail wagging madly as they walked to the back door. In the kitchen, Theo's keys made a clinking sound as he dropped them on to the granite-topped bench. Then there was silence.

And, out of the blue, Annie found herself rushing to speak at last, to say something... *anything*. 'Are you hungry?'

'Hungry?'

'My brothers are always starving when they come home from cocktail parties. As far as they're concerned, canapés aren't real food and they always complain that they can never get enough to eat.'

Theo looked mildly surprised. 'I guess we could have some supper.'

'Would you like something light? Scrambled eggs, perhaps?'

'That sounds—er—fine.'

While Annie busied herself finding eggs and milk and a saucepan, he took off his coat, re-moved his bow-tie and loosened his collar. She dashed out into the courtyard and snipped some parsley and chives from the potted herbs and returned to find Theo observing her assem-bled ingredients with a puzzled frown.

'Shall I put on some music?' she asked.

'Yes, whatever you like.'

Without stopping to choose, she grabbed a CD from the stack and slipped it into the player and next minute the slow, sexy sounds of a romantic ballad rippled around them. *What a dumb, dumb selection.*

As she turned back to the bench she felt so tense she thought she might crack in two.

'Annie.' Theo came up behind her. She was holding an egg and his hand closed gently over hers. 'Are you really hungry?'

She almost crushed the fragile eggshell as she turned to face him. 'No. I mean, yes. Well, I just thought—'

What was the matter with her? This wasn't the way tonight was supposed to happen. Everything was turning out wrong, wrong, *wrong.*

He smiled slowly, took the egg from her grasp and set it back in the bowl with the others. 'Why on earth are we making scrambled eggs when neither of us is hungry?'

'I—I—because I suggested it, I guess. I—thought perhaps—'

He placed a finger against her lips. A finger that was strong, confident, capable. Perfect.

Her heart thumped so loudly she was sure he must hear it.

'Let's forget supper,' he said.

She nodded.

Holding her by the shoulders, he let his thumbs trace the line of her collarbones. 'I'm afraid this attraction thing isn't going away. Not for me, at any rate.'

'No, not for me, either.'

His fingers traced back and forth over her shoulders, following the superfine silken straps. 'All evening I've been wanting to tell you how incredible you look. This *naked shimmer* is a major distraction for me.'

Now she could feel her heart thumping in her chest and in a pulse in her throat. 'That's what I was hoping when I bought it.' Crikey, that sounded much, much braver than she felt.

'So—you planned to seduce me?'

'Yes, I—um—toyed with the idea.'

His face broke into one of his lovely smiles. 'I must say I like the way your mind works, Annie McKinnon.'

Then, dropping his hands to her waist, he tested the texture of the shimmering fabric. His hands spanned her ribs and he lowered his head till their lips touched. He teased her with a hardly-there brush of his mouth over hers and Annie hoped he didn't mind that she seemed to be shaking.

Apparently not. Next minute his hands cradled her face and he kissed her properly, and his lips were slow, soft and tantalising. Swoon-worthy.

'So this attraction thing…' he murmured. 'Want to do something about it?'

'Yes… I do.'

Annie was definitely trembling now and there was every chance her knees might give way, but the next minute Theo lifted her up in his arms.

Goodness, this was the sort of caveman stunt a man like her brothers might have pulled, but she hadn't expected anything so macho from Theo. 'I'm too heavy!'

Ignoring her protests, he carried her across the kitchen, through the lounge, to the stairs.

'Not the stairs, Theo. You can't. You'll strain something.'

Without any sign of strain, he carried her up the stairs and into his room.

His room.

The room with the sumptuous bed, the rich cream bedspread and the tumble of black and cream silk cushions. The glow of timber shutters closed against the night. Lamplight.

And Theo.

Theo, lowering her on to his bed, then joining her and kissing her some more. She let her eyes drift closed as he kissed her slowly, lazily, as if he had all the time in the world for nothing but kisses. She surrendered with total complicity to the leisurely caress of his sensuous lips, to the playful flirtation of his gentle little bites, and the arousing dance of his tongue meeting and mating with hers.

The last of her nervousness melted away as she luxuriated in the warmth of his unhurried, easy seduction.

'You have the most gorgeous mouth,' he murmured.

'Your kisses are sensational,' she whispered back.

He kissed some more while his hands traced slow, circling patterns on her shoulders and up and down her arms. Beneath his easy touch her body turned languid and warm. Why had she ever been nervous? This was Theo and he was perfect. He knew exactly what was right for her.

Then he stole her breath as his hand slipped lower to caress her thighs. A flowering of longing spilled deep inside her and suddenly she was impatient to feel his touch all over.

She gasped. 'I've got to get out of this dress.'

A surprised little laugh escaped him as she rolled into a sitting position.

'Can you undo my zip?'

Theo obliged, and she wriggled in a frantic attempt to shed her clothing.

'Whoa, Annie, don't tear your dress. It's too lovely to wreck the first time you wear it.'

She raised her hands over her head. 'Can you help?'

Theo could. And she watched in a fever of anticipation as he carried her dress across the room and draped it carefully over the chair in the corner, but when he removed his own clothes he let them fall to the floor without paying them any attention.

His attention was for Annie.

And she couldn't drag her eyes from him. He was everything she'd ever wanted in a man. Her heart pounded, her skin burned, her body yearned for his.

His eyes paid homage to her as he moved back on to the bed, and everything in her world became perfect when his lips found hers once more. His hands began to glide down her arms, over the bumps of her hips, into the dip of her waist and then to the swell of her breasts.

And she explored him the way he was touching her, tracing the wonderfully muscular contours of his shoulders, the smooth sweep of his back, the hair on his chest. Then lower.

With each kiss, each tender touch, their hunger mounted and their sense of intimacy deepened. Sweet, poignant longing coiled and built inside her, making her body arch with pleasure. She felt heavy-limbed and anchored by desire and yet blissfully free, happy that the soft, needy little sounds that escaped her would let Theo know how much she loved his touch, was grateful for each daring caress.

And her eagerness released a new kind of wildness in them both. The tempo of their lovemaking changed as Theo's gentle, lazy seduction gave way to focused passion.

Annie whispered his name and he whispered hers back to her, turning her name into a breathless caress as he murmured it over and over, until at last the words were lost inside one long, hungry kiss before they were both swept beyond recall—hot-blooded lovers drowning in a flood of desperate need.

Theo lay in the stillness of midnight, in the slanted moonlight that stole through the shutters, with Annie's head resting against his chest and her soft breath warm on his skin, and he waited for regret to attack him.

He had every reason to feel remorse. He had just made love to a woman who was almost certainly too young and trusting for an uncommitted, casual relationship. Annie McKinnon was the kind of girl who needed to believe that the act of sex was an act of commitment. An act of faith.

Now, as she slept, he threaded his fingers through the soft golden strands of her hair and examined his motives again and again, searching for blame.

But the search was in vain. Although Theo tormented himself with self-recrimination, he had absolutely no sense of regret. Sane, logical reason and theories about incompatibility simply refused to stack up against the overwhelming force of his feelings.

With Annie tonight, he'd felt a helpless tenderness and a depth of emotion that made absolute nonsense of theory and reason. Perhaps he'd lost his head, but he'd found his heart. And while common sense pointed to the fact that tonight had been an error of judgement, something far deeper told Theo Grainger that it was quite possible he'd made a deliberate choice and that the passion he'd shared with Annie McKinnon was neither casual nor uncommitted.

Which led him to one surprising conclusion.

It was quite, quite possible that he was falling in love with her. And nothing about it felt like a mistake.

CHAPTER EIGHT

BREAKFAST next morning was lazy, luxurious...and late.

Basil missed out on his early walk while Annie and Theo stayed in bed. It was almost mid-morning before they wandered downstairs.

Theo didn't seem to be in a rush to get to work and he was more than happy to hang around while Annie made a special breakfast of pancakes with strawberries and cream.

Sitting in the courtyard under a smiling sky, they took time over coffee, stealing kisses that tasted of strawberries, and basking as only new lovers can in the warmth of their exquisite happiness.

They talked about happiness. Their happiness. About whether Basil, who was stretched blissfully over their feet, could sense their happiness. And was it possible for dogs to ever be as happy as Annie and Theo were right now, on this bright, beautiful, beaming morning?

Neither of them dared to suggest that the

state of happiness could be slippery—that happiness could slide from beneath your feet when you least expected it.

'What's the Italian word for happiness?' Annie asked instead.

'*Felicità.*'

'Oh, I like that. Italian always sounds so amazingly sexy.'

They might have spent ages talking and gently flirting, just as they'd spent ages making love last night and again that morning, but eventually Theo looked at his watch and sighed. 'I had better get to work.'

'I'll take Basil for his walk,' she volunteered.

'It won't hurt him to miss a day.'

'No, but I'd like to take him. I need to walk off these pancakes so I have room for lunch with Mel.'

Theo made a teasing comment about ladies who lunch and they kissed some more, before he left.

Mel took one look at Annie and gasped. 'Omigosh, it's happened, hasn't it?'

'What?'

It took several seconds of panic before Annie reassured herself that it wasn't possible for the whole world to guess what she'd been doing last night just by looking at her. Just the same, the knowing gleam in Mel's eyes brought a rush of embarrassment. And she blushed.

'You're up to your eyebrows in love,' Mel said.

'It shows?'

'Of course it shows, Annie. Your glow is bright enough to light up the Power House.'

There wasn't much point in trying to pretend otherwise, so she nodded.

'And?' Mel prompted.

'And what?'

'And what about Theo? Is he wrapped, too?'

'It…it seems…yes, I think he is, Mel.'

'Wow, Annie, scoring with Dr Theo is such a coup.'

Annie drew a deep breath. A coup? Scoring? Was that what she'd done? Surely not. Making love with Theo had felt ever so much more special than notching up points in some kind of competition.

She made an unnecessary show of studying the menu. 'Are you having a salad, Mel?'

''Fraid so. I don't dare have anything else. One of the guys at work has invited me to a gala ball next month and I'm trying to lose weight so I can squeeze into something red and strapless.'

'A guy at work?' Annie seized on the chance to divert attention from herself. 'Come on, tell me more.'

To her relief, Mel was happy to explain about Bill Brown, a cute, lanky, thirty-something guy in Planning. And then Mel went on to tell Annie about Victoria's latest foray into the heady world of speed-dating and their girl talk steered into safer, Theo-free waters.

It wasn't till near the end of their lunch that Mel said, 'So what happens next, Annie? Are you still going home to North Queensland next week, or are you planning to move in permanently with Theo?'

'If everything works out, I won't be going back to Southern Cross,' Annie said and then she felt a slam of shock as she realised how easy it was to make such an astonishing statement.

The days that followed were pure magic. First there was the weekend. Two whole days with Theo's undivided attention; two days to explore Brisbane together.

'Your enthusiasm is like a tonic,' he told her. 'I love seeing my home town through your eyes.'

After his return to work on Monday, Annie

took Basil for extra walks, or pottered about the house and courtyard garden. She continued her exploration of the galleries, and in the evenings she talked with Theo about what she'd discovered.

It was pretty phenomenal the way she'd morphed so easily into a lust-pot. But Theo's transformation was just as dramatic. It was hard to believe this amazing, red-hot lover was the same polite, rather formal 'uncle' she'd met such a short time ago.

It was almost like waking up in one of those perfume commercials where a girl used a certain scent and suddenly there was a guy who needed to chase her with a bunch of flowers or murmur nonsense in her ear at the oddest moments, just because he loved the smell of her.

And then there was the soul mate thing. It kind of got shoved aside in the heat of passion, but it crept in at other times. Annie couldn't get enough of talking with Theo. They talked about *everything* and she was as crazy about his mind as she was about his body. And his smile.

And the most fabulous thing was that Theo was absolutely committed to discovering the real Annie. She'd never met anyone so interested in *her* thoughts. He was intrigued by her past, her reactions to the present and her dreams for the future. She felt totally flattered.

'Tell me more about your home at Southern Cross,' he said one evening as she lay beside him in a stream of silver starlight.

'What would you like to know?'

'Do you have a favourite haunt?'

'Lots.'

'Any special place that you escape to when you want to be on your own?'

'Yes, there's a spot down by the creek.'

Drawing her close, he pressed a warm kiss into the curve of her neck. 'Tell me about it. I'd like to picture it. Shut your eyes and go there in your mind. Describe it to me.'

With her eyes closed, she snuggled more comfortably against him. 'Okay. I'm sitting on the creek bank.'

'A high bank?'

'Yes, a reasonably high, grassy bank with clumps of reeds growing down near the water's edge. The water is dark green and still. You wouldn't think it was moving at all, but there's a leaf floating past very slowly. And there are little water spiders dimpling the surface.' She turned to him. 'They make little circular ripples all over the top of the water.'

He nodded. 'And is the water very clear?'

'Yes, you can see through it to mossy logs on the bottom.'

'Sounds lovely. What else?'

'Well...there are lily pads all along the edge of the creek with tiny white flowers. And there's a melaleuca tree on the opposite bank with branches leaning right out, low over the water at an impossible angle, and you half-expect the tree to topple into the creek. And...there's a tangle of lantana bushes and a small wattle with yellow flowers that really stand out against all the green. And right on the top of the bank there are massive eucalypt trees towering up to the sky.'

'Is it quiet there?'

'Yes, absolutely.'

'Can you hear anything?'

'Mmm...every so often there's a breeze that runs up the creek and you hear the sound of it whispering through the treetops.'

'Birds?'

'A peaceful dove. Honey-eaters. Chip chips.'

He lifted a curl from her forehead and kissed her brow. 'Annie, are you quite sure you're not missing the bush?'

His face was in shadow, but she thought she heard a throaty tension in his voice. She rubbed her cheek against the smooth cradle of his shoulder. 'I'm sure, Theo. I love the bush and I guess it will always be my home, and I'll be happy to go back to visit, but I've never felt I belonged there the way my brothers do. Lately, I've felt as if the outback was stifling me. I *needed* to escape. Damien was just an excuse. I was already desperate for a city life.'

He seemed content with that.

After a bit, Annie rolled on to her tummy and poked his shoulder. 'Your turn,' she said.

He mumbled sleepily.

'Come on, tell me one of your favourite places. Tell me about somewhere in Italy.'

'Which city?'

'I don't mind. It's all exciting to me.'

'Give me a kiss first.'

Annie was happy to oblige.

'Okay, I'll describe the view from the apartment I rented when I was studying in Rome. It's in an ancient quarter called Trastevere, the place where musicians, writers and artists from all over the world like to stay—a bit like Greenwich Village in New York.'

'It sounds wonderful. Are you looking out of a window?'

'Yes.' With his arms around her, he spoke softly in his lovely deep voice. 'I've opened the shutters and it's early. The light is still soft—and in the distance I can see the rounded outline of a hill with cypresses and umbrella pines silhouetted against the sky.'

She felt an unexpected thrill as if she were there with him. She could see it all. 'What about the buildings?'

'Oh, there are plenty of them. I can see sloping, tiled rooftops, television aerials, spires and domes. There are ancient temples and Roman ruins crowding shoulder to shoulder with modern architecture. And if I look straight below me, I see a little cobbled piazza.'

'Oh, wow! What else? Can you see any people?'

'An old man sitting on the steps in front of a small fountain. A fellow putting up umbrellas on the tables outside a café. And another man opening up his news-stand.'

'Where are the women? Still in bed?'

Theo laughed. 'There's a woman watering her geraniums and herbs on a little balcony.'

'Can you smell anything?'

'Freshly baked bread and pizza.'

'Oh, yum. It sounds truly amazing, Theo.'

'It is.'

'I'd love to see it one day.'

'I'll take you there.'

Another wild thrill sent her sitting bolt upright. 'You really mean that?'

'Yes,' he said, sounding almost as surprised as she was. 'I really do.'

On the days she took Basil for bonus walks Annie liked to explore the streets closer to Theo's place, where humble, old-fashioned workers' cottages were still scattered among the modern townhouses and apartment blocks.

Friendly, elderly folk lived in the cottages, she noticed. Several were sitting on their front porches or working in their front gardens when she passed, and they smiled and nodded to her the way people in Mirrabrook did.

She felt almost at home.

That was how she met George.

She saw the elderly man leaning on his front gate as she walked down his street and she smiled and called, 'Good morning.'

He returned her greeting with a wave and suddenly Basil charged towards him, straining on the leash, his tail wagging madly.

'Hello, Basil, old mate,' the man said, leaning down to give the top of the Dalmatian's head an affectionate scruff.

'Do you two know each other?' Annie asked.

'We sure do.' He beamed broadly. 'I'm Basil's grandfather.'

Annie laughed, but her laugh turned into an

exclamation of surprise as she watched the delirious way Basil responded to the old man. *Basil's grandfather?* It was obvious these two knew each other very well. Did that mean…?

Recognising her confusion, he grinned again. 'I'm George Grainger, Theo's father.'

'Oh, my.' She stared at him in amazement. It had never occurred to her that Theo's father might live so close by. 'So you're Pop?'

'That's right.'

'Well—how nice.'

'And you must be Annie.'

'You've heard about me?'

'Of course I have, love. From Damien and from Theo.' He shook her proffered hand. 'How do you do?'

'I'm very pleased to meet you, Mr Grainger.'

Now that she looked more carefully, she could see the likeness to both Theo and Damien. George Grainger was shorter, probably because he was a little stooped, and his hair was white, his face lined and his knuckles knobbly with arthritis, but behind his glasses his eyes were the same alert hazel as his son's and grandson's.

And he was looking at her with an intense interest that bordered on delight.

'How is Damien?' she asked, wondering exactly what George had been told about her connection to his son and his grandson.

'Right as rain,' he said. 'He's at work this morning.' Then he surprised her by unlatching his gate and swinging it open. 'Why don't you come on in, Annie?'

Basil pulled frantically on the leash in an effort to dive through the gateway. 'Looks like Basil loves coming here,' she said, giving in.

'We're old mates. I'm his favourite ear-scratcher and I look after him whenever Theo goes away.'

Annie wondered what Theo would think if he could see her following his father down a shady path that took them around the side of his simple weatherboard cottage to a sunny back garden filled with plots of vegetables.

'Wow! These are doing well,' she said, looking around at staked tomato plants, rows of corn, silverbeet, carrots and lettuce. 'You must have a wonderful green thumb.'

He nodded, smiling. 'Gardening keeps me active.' Then he added, 'This was Theo's home when he was a boy, you know.'

'No, I didn't,' she said. 'So he's lived in this part of Brisbane all his life?'

'Yep. Apart from the couple of semesters he's spent studying overseas. He bought the town house around the corner when his mother took ill, so he could stay in close contact. We lost her four years ago.'

'I'm sorry.'

'He's a good son.'

Annie tried to picture Theo here, growing up with his sister and parents in this tiny cottage, and she felt a touch embarrassed. What must a man from George Grainger's generation think of a young woman who'd moved in with his son—who'd *slept* with his son—after such a short acquaintance?

'You're probably wondering why Damien moved out,' she said.

'Theo explained,' George assured her. 'He popped in last week to check whether Damien arrived here and he filled me in. His version was a little different from Damien's, of course.'

She would have loved to ask what George Grainger had been told, but refrained.

'Would you like a cool drink?' George looked at her eagerly, almost pleading with her to say yes. 'Come along inside. Basil will be happy to lie here in the sun.'

'Thank you,' she said, recognising the loneliness behind his request. She'd experienced her share of loneliness at Southern Cross. 'But I mustn't stay long.'

In the kitchen he invited her to sit at a small

wooden table painted a fresh mint green and he took a jug from the refrigerator and poured her a glass of old-fashioned lemon and barley water.

She looked around her and thought about Theo being here in this kitchen every day of his boyhood, eating breakfast at this table. She could imagine him coming in from playing outside and forgetting to wipe his feet, raiding the old pottery cookie jar, reading with a torch after lights out in a little bedroom down the hallway.

She remembered to take a sip of her drink. 'This is delicious, Mr Grainger.'

'Call me George,' he said and he smiled and began to ask her about her home in the outback.

Ten minutes later, she realised she'd told him a potted history of almost everything about herself—about her brothers, their cattle property, her years at boarding school, her father's death and her mother's return to Scotland. She'd even confessed about her loneliness—and meeting Damien over the Internet.

'You must miss your mother,' he said.

'Yes.' She drew a deep breath and tried to ignore the little niggle of hurt she felt whenever she remembered how easily her mother had resettled on the other side of the world.

George's keen eyes watched her for a moment or two, but when she didn't volunteer anything else about her mother he told her stories about Theo—about what a terrific Rugby Union player he'd been, representing Queensland during his undergraduate days. And what a brilliant student he'd been. George confessed that he and his wife had never understood how they'd produced such a clever son—and then he added details of how wonderfully well Theo had looked after Damien.

Annie would have happily stayed on with George. Between them they could have formed a Theo Grainger Admiration Society, but she had promised to meet Mel again for lunch, and so eventually she made her excuses.

George accompanied her as she collected Basil. 'Come and visit me again,' he said.

'I'd love to,' she promised.

At the front gate he said simply, 'You're the one, Annie.'

'Th-the one?'

His eyes shone shyly. 'The one I've been waiting for Theo to find.'

She felt a bright blush burning her cheeks. 'You've shocked me, George. I don't know what to say.'

'I'm sorry,' he said. 'I know that was very forward of me. I'm a silly old man. But don't

worry, I won't make trouble by saying anything to Theo.' He bent down and patted
Basil's head. 'I don't reckon I'll have to. Do
you, mate? Not if Theo's as smart as he makes
out.'

Driving home to Annie with a bright bouquet
of flowers on the seat beside him, a bottle of
expensive wine stowed in the glove box and
tubs of aromatic Thai take-away packed in a
box on the floor, Theo was comfortably confident that all was right with his world.

He'd rung Annie mid-afternoon, but she'd
still been out, so he'd left a message on the
answering machine telling her not to worry
about preparing dinner. He'd briefly toyed
with the idea of taking her out to a restaurant—to La Piastra perhaps—but he was still
feeling too selfish to share her with a room full
of people.

That was what infatuation did to a guy.
Theo wanted, no, needed, to be alone with
Annie. At home. Just the two of them. All
night.

He pictured how it would be when he
walked into the kitchen this evening. Pictured
the way Annie's face would light up when she
saw the flowers. She was so delightfully ap-
preciative of the smallest gestures and she

never held back in expressing her pleasure. Her eyes, her face, her whole body responded.

Her uncomplicated spontaneity was contagious. Theo had caught himself whistling at work a couple of times this week. Whistling, for heaven's sake. And his extravagant outbursts of cheerfulness had not gone unnoticed by the staff.

However, he couldn't be bothered about the wry glances of colleagues and their cryptic comments about his *Ode to Joy*. He was almost home.

And, as he thought of home, he recognised another dramatic shift in his thinking. Already he'd begun to suppose that Annie belonged in his home. The idea of her leaving to return to the wilds of North Queensland appalled him. He must make sure she understood how much he wanted her to stay.

He wanted to introduce her to his father, too. The two of them were sure to hit it off. He'd even begun to consider contingency plans for Damien's future. It was too much to expect old George to care for his grandson indefinitely and Damien's mother was still tied up with her job in Sydney.

But Damien would be attending UQ next year... Perhaps he would enjoy a year in a student residential college? Living on campus with other students would be good for him. St John's College would suit him down to the ground…and Theo had good connections there.

Pleased with that possibility, he smiled as his car rounded the corner into his street. But his smile and his musings were zapped instantly by the sight of a dark green sedan parked in front of his house.

Claudia.

What on earth was she doing here?

Theo wasn't given to overreaction, or to fanciful notions of telepathy, or premonitions for that matter, but at the sight of Claudia's car a voice in his head whispered a distinct and chilling warning.

He scowled as he parked his car in the garage. How long had Claudia been here? And how was Annie handling her visit?

His scowl sharpened as he anticipated Claudia's cynical reaction to his arrival with his arms full of telling purchases, and he almost left the flowers behind on the car seat but sudden loyalty to Annie changed his mind.

Claudia could make of them whatever she wished.

The two women were sitting in the courtyard drinking wine and as soon as Claudia spotted him she waved and called hello.

He crossed the lawn and saw that the wine was one of her favourites. Almost certainly she'd brought it with her.

'Oh, what a charming picture,' Claudia said as he drew nearer. 'Those flowers suit you beautifully, Theo. You should carry bouquets more often.'

'Hello, Claudia.' He tried to inject a degree of polite welcome into his voice but it fell rather flat.

Turning to Annie, he offered his warmest smile. 'Hi, there,' he said softly. 'How was lunch?'

'*Lunch* was lovely,' Annie said with a subtle emphasis on the first word and a quick glance that implied that things had gone rapidly downhill since then. 'What gorgeous lilies, Theo.'

'I'll take everything through to the kitchen and then I'll grab a glass and join you,' he said.

To his surprise, Claudia jumped to her feet. 'I'll come inside too, Theo. There's something I need to discuss with you.'

A steel band seemed to clamp around his chest.

'A business matter,' Claudia said, averting her eyes momentarily before sighing significantly. 'I'm afraid I have some rather bad news.'

A grim kind of dread settled inside him. He had no idea what was going on, but nothing about Claudia's visit felt right.

Determined to remain calm, he allowed himself a small frown. 'Couldn't you have shared this bad news with me at work?'

'I was held up in meetings all afternoon.' Claudia lifted her gaze slowly. 'And then I couldn't find you. You must have been out hunting for these delightful purchases.' Her mouth flickered into a smile that was too thin, almost cruel. 'But because we're old friends I didn't want to leave you in the dark, so I came straight here. I'd hate you to find out from anyone else.'

'What don't you want me to find out, Claudia? For God's sake, what's happened?'

She cast a speaking glance in Annie's direction, and Theo saw that Annie's cheeks were flushed and her eyes worried.

'I need to discuss this with you in private,' Claudia said.

'You had better come into my study then.' He struggled to hold back a mounting sense of alarm. 'Please excuse us, Annie.'

*   *   *

Annie felt sick as she placed Theo's bottle of white wine in the fridge and put the tubs of food in the microwave and then arranged his flowers in a tall rectangular glass vase and carried them through to the lounge. The flowers were gorgeous, long-stemmed lilies—deep red, golden and cream—and they teamed beautifully with the colours and mood of this room.

But she couldn't enjoy them. Not when she could hear the sombre murmur of voices from behind the closed door of Theo's study.

Setting the vase on the coffee table, she made a few adjustments to the arrangement, but as she straightened she found herself stalled in the middle of the room, hypnotised by the threat of those muffled voices. She wound her arms across her stomach, as if to protect herself.

Perhaps it was pathetically paranoid of her, but she knew just knew that this bad news of Claudia's was somehow linked to her.

The half hour she'd spent alone with Claudia before Theo had arrived home had been hideous. Claudia had feigned an interest in Annie's life in North Queensland, but her boredom had been thinly veiled and when Annie tried to talk about Brisbane or the university Claudia's manner had been patronising in the extreme.

Without actually saying so, the other woman had conveyed with crystalline clarity that she couldn't imagine how dear, clever Theo had become infatuated with such a brainless little bimbo from the back of beyond. It had taken all Annie's self-control to refrain from acquainting Claudia with the truly astonishing fact that the Star Valley was not populated by a mob of inbred, illiterate, banjo-playing yokels.

The voices in the study stopped abruptly and Annie hurried back to the kitchen, terrified that it might look as if she'd been eavesdropping.

Basil was sprawled on the back step and she crossed the room and dropped on to the step beside him. Seeking comfort, she gave him a huge hug. 'If only you could tell me what you know about Claudia,' she whispered to the dog. 'Has she been here often? Is she in love with Theo? What do you think is going on in there?'

Basil pushed his wet nose against her neck and gave her a loving lick. He made a gentle, whimpering sound as if he were trying to comfort her. 'You dear old boy,' she said, rubbing her cheek against his magnificent black and white spotted neck. 'You understand, don't you?'

'You really do get on well with Basil, don't you?'

Annie jumped at the sound of Claudia's

voice. She hadn't heard footsteps. Whipping around, she was startled to see the other woman standing in the kitchen behind her. She shot a quick glance past her, hoping to see Theo, but there was no sign of him.

She jumped to her feet. 'Have you and Theo finished your discussion?'

'Yes.' Claudia fished in her handbag and extracted her car keys. 'I imagine you'll want to go inside and offer the poor man some comfort.'

Horrified, Annie whispered, 'W—what's happened?'

'I've had to let him go.'

'Let him go?' Annie felt ill. 'What on earth do you mean?'

'Theo's contract as a lecturer was up for renewal at the end of this year, but our department has had severe funding cuts and we were left with a very difficult decision.'

Annie gasped. 'You can't mean that he's lost his job?'

'Believe me, Annie, it's a grave disappointment for all of us. But I can imagine how distressed you particularly must feel. I saw how hard you tried to fit in at the soirée last week. I'm terribly sorry but all that's going to be lost to you now.'

Appalled, Annie stared at her, unable to think of anything to say.

Claudia's long, nimble fingers sorted through her key ring and she made a selection. Tapping the key against her elegant chin, she eyed Annie thoughtfully. 'I'm sorry if you feel badly about this.'

'Well, of course I feel badly. I feel terrible for Theo.'

Claudia looked pained, then she shook her head and rolled her eyes before releasing an impatient, huffing sigh.

'What is it?' challenged Annie, too fraught to decide whether this woman was displaying an Oscar-winning performance or genuine emotion. 'Is there something I'm supposed to understand? Something else I should feel bad about?'

Claudia turned as if she were leaving, then looked back at Annie and said almost gently, 'You don't see the problem, do you, Annie?'

Annie felt a terrible urge to slap her. 'I might if you gave me a clue.'

Again Claudia sighed. 'Sometimes we don't want to accept that we might be a burden or a hindrance to people we're very fond of.'

'A—a burden?' Annie's legs threatened to buckle beneath her. 'Are you telling me this is m-my fault? Theo's losing his job because of me?'

The brief but unmistakable flash of triumph in Claudia's eyes indicated that this was the exact message she'd intended.

'How can I be a hindrance to Theo's career? I only met him a week ago.'

But now Claudia chose not to answer. She'd planted the necessary seeds. Without another word, she turned and walked purposefully out of the house without looking back.

A wave of nausea swept through Annie. This didn't make sense. How could she have caused so much havoc in Theo's life in such a short space of time?

She thought of last week at the cocktail party, and remembered her dress and the silly comment about naked shimmer. She remembered the way Theo had kissed her hand in full view of everyone, and the way he'd stolen away early with her...

No doubt a few tongues had wagged, but surely in this day and age something like that didn't amount to a scandal? Not the kind of scandal that got a man sacked. *Unless*...

From the street outside came the sound of Claudia's car starting up. Last week Annie had suspected that Claudia and Theo had a past relationship. Now she was almost certain of it.

And she was just as certain that Claudia wasn't over Theo.

CHAPTER NINE

HEARTSICK, Annie hurried through the house to Theo's study. He was sitting in a black leather chair with his elbows propped on the desk, his head slumped in his hands.

She stopped in the doorway. Although she wanted to run to him, to throw her arms around him and to comfort him, Claudia's words had undermined her confidence.

Had she really cost Theo his job? Her throat burned with a painful, rocky clump of mounting fear. Fisting a hand against her mouth to stop herself from making a noise, she drew a deep breath, trying to calm down. The last thing Theo needed was hysterics from her. For the moment, until she heard his side of the story, she would have to be strong and put Claudia's accusations behind her.

It was growing dark outside and the only light in the study came from the lamp on Theo's desk. In spite of her agitation, she couldn't help admiring his bowed head—the dark sheen of his hair in the lamp's light and the neat, essentially masculine way his hair ended in a straight line across the back of his neck.

What am I going to do? I'm so in love with this man. I couldn't bear to walk away from him now.

After a minute or two he lowered his hands and looked up, surprised to see her there. 'Hi,' he said. 'I didn't hear you.'

She stepped into the room. 'Theo, I'm so sorry.'

'Claudia told you?'

'Yes, it's terrible.'

He sighed. 'I must admit I'm feeling a bit shell-shocked.' Then he smiled faintly and said, 'Come here.'

Moving closer, Annie hitched a hip on to the edge of his desk and leaned forward to touch her fingers lightly against his cheekbone. The little laughter creases around his eyes looked as if they'd been etched deeper by pain. He was hurt more than he was letting on and she couldn't bear it.

'I don't understand, Theo. How can the university do this to you?'

'Very easily, it would seem.'

'But how can they dump news like this out of the blue, without warning?'

He shrugged. 'Normally a lecturer would

have some idea that a contract might not be renewed, but it's still legitimate for it to happen as quickly as this.'

'It might be legitimate, but it's too cruel.' When he didn't respond she couldn't help adding, 'Why was Claudia the one to tell you?'

'She's the head of the department.'

'Really?' She couldn't hold back a choked cry of dismay. 'Claudia's your boss?'

'Yes.' He saw the look on her face and added, 'She's a highly intelligent, very qualified academic, Annie.'

She sniffed. 'Maybe she is, but there was nothing high-minded or ethical about the way she sacked you.'

'I'm sure she would argue that she conducted herself in a very civilised manner.'

Annie shook her head and almost snarled.

'Don't look so worried, Annie. I'll be okay. Losing a job isn't the end of the world.'

She might have guessed that Theo would be stoical about such an unexpected disappointment. 'I'm more angry than worried,' she said and she had to compress her lips to stop herself from saying more. Would Theo think her suspicions about Claudia were catty?

But it was impossible for impetuous Annie McKinnon to hold back for long. Moments later the question that burned inside her burst out. 'Is Claudia in love with you, Theo?'

He let out a little huff of surprise and looked away quickly. 'Of course not.'

'Do you and she have a history?' She pressed her hand against the burning knot of panic in her stomach.

His eyes were worried as he turned back to her. His hand sought hers. 'Yes, but it was over long ago. Almost two years ago now.'

'I wouldn't be too sure that it's over.'

'Believe me, Annie. Claudia and I are *ancient* history.'

'You may think so, Theo, but I suspect Claudia is still hung up on you. I think it's very possible that what happened today was the green-eyed monster in action.'

He frowned and shook his head. 'Claudia's above that.'

Oh, boy. He had no idea.

He knew nothing of the half hour she'd spent squirming in Claudia's unpleasant company. Annie was sure the woman could stoop to murky depths if it suited her. 'I'm sorry, Theo, but I can't agree with you. Claudia might have top credentials, but I don't believe she's a philosopher's boot lace.'

A corner of his mouth twitched upwards. 'What makes you say that?'

'If she was trying to think rationally and logically and for the greater good, why would she choose to get rid of one of her most valuable lecturers?'

'You don't know anything about my value at work.'

'Yes, I do. People were falling over themselves last week to tell me what a popular and effective lecturer you are.' She dropped a quick kiss on his cheek, then slipped from the desk and walked quickly away from him.

I mustn't cry. I mustn't cry. Hunching her shoulders, she wrapped her arms over her stomach and she kept her back to him as she stared through a long, narrow window to the dusky outline of a lipstick palm growing in the courtyard.

'This sacking has nothing to do with the quality of your teaching.' A sob threatened and she gulped it down. 'It's about me, Theo. *I'm* your problem.'

'For God's sake, Annie, *no*!'

The shocked pain in his voice almost tore her in two. *Claudia hadn't said anything to him.*

It made sense. Claudia was too smart to openly point to Annie as the reason for Theo's dismissal. And he, poor lamb, didn't have the benefit of feminine intuition, so he probably hadn't noticed that haunted watchfulness in Claudia's eyes whenever she looked at him. And he hadn't heard the lethal parting shot his boss had fired at Annie.

'I'm afraid it's true.' With her back to him, Annie drew a deep breath and once again willed herself not to cry. 'If I left you, you'd have your job back in no time.'

Close behind her now, Theo clasped her by the elbows. 'That's not how it works.'

At his touch she almost sobbed aloud. She closed her eyes to hold back the tears, but the telltale moisture slid from beneath her lashes and down her cheeks.

Theo hauled her backwards hard against him. 'Don't even think of leaving me.' Binding her with his arms, he pressed hot kisses to the back of her neck.

She was helpless, overcome by heartbreak. She didn't want to go…didn't want to…didn't want to. And Theo was holding her so tightly, he was kissing her hair, her wet cheek, her neck.

'This is not your fault,' he whispered.

But she knew it was. It *was* her fault. She was the reason Theo had lost his job. Nevertheless, when he whispered, 'Come here,' she turned in his arms, powerless to resist him as he covered her damp face with kisses.

'I want you in my life, Annie.'

Oh, Theo. Lovely, lovely Theo.

Cradling her face, he kissed her mouth. And she was lost, lost on the riding tide of her emotions, on a cresting wave of despair and longing.

Later she would think about what she must do to get Theo's job back, but not now. Not now when he was kissing her with a tenderness that blocked all sensible thought. Not now when his hands and his mouth left her no choice but to submit to sensation...when they were both trembling with the accelerating force of their feelings.

Not now when he was undoing the buttons of her blouse...when she was undoing the snap fastener at the waist of her jeans...when he was peeling her blouse away from her shoulders, when his lips were tracing the lacy patterns on her bra...while she tugged his shirt free from his trousers...

Only this...now...

The future and the past vanished and they let the urgency of the present take them by storm, expressing their emotions in the most honest and intimate way, the only way possible now.

All that mattered was this moment…and their sensitivity to each other's touch. Nothing else counted but their heightening need…the act of giving and receiving…and their rapturous, passionate drive for completion.

And afterwards…after they'd dressed again and after they'd giggled as they gathered and sorted the papers that had fallen from Theo's desk and scattered all over the study…after they'd heated the Thai take-away and poured fresh glasses of wine and eaten their dinner, picnic style on the floor of the lounge, and admired the lilies on the coffee table…

After all this, Theo still refused to accept that his dismissal had anything to do with Annie. And, because she couldn't bear to start a fight with him, she let the matter drop. For now.

'What will you do?' she asked as they carried the take-away cartons back to the kitchen.

'The only thing I can do. Look around for a new job.'

'But will there be another job like yours going in Brisbane?'

'It's highly unlikely. Actually, I'm almost certain there won't be anything on offer here for next semester.'

'But if you have to go away, what will happen to Damien? And George? He'll be terribly disappointed.'

'George?' Theo's eyebrows became question marks.

'Your father. You know that nice elderly gentleman who lives in the little white cottage around the corner?'

'But—' He smiled and frowned simultaneously, clearly puzzled. 'How do you know about him?'

Annie smiled back. 'I met him today when I took Basil for his walk.'

'Did you, now? So you've been spying behind my back?'

'It was more like the inaugural meeting of the Theo Grainger Fan Club.'

Theo grinned. 'What a charming idea.'

It was the first time he'd grinned all evening. 'I could scrounge up a few more members,' she said, hoping to cheer him some more. *Everyone who knows you loves you, Theo.* 'My friend Victoria was smitten at first sight.' Remembering the Italian café owner she'd met on the first morning, she added, 'I'm sure Giovanni would join us if he was invited.'

'Perhaps they will write me a good reference,' Theo said, with a grimace that was more rueful than cheerful.

You won't need a reference, Theo. Not when I've done what I have to do.

But at the thought of the task that awaited her in the morning, Annie shuddered.

'What's the matter?' he asked.

She forced a weak smile. 'I just wish this hadn't happened.'

'It'll turn out all right. I'm going to look on this as a challenge, a new bend in the road. Who knows what I'll find waiting around the corner?'

'Now you're being philosophical.'

'Of course. Why not?'

'Because this should never have happened. It's unfair.' She caught the quizzical expression in Theo's eyes and shook her head. 'I know, I know, we can't expect life to always be fair.'

Just the same… She looked around her at Theo's lovely home. It would be a wrench for him to leave it. She thought of Damien, who still needed his uncle's guidance, of George, Theo's ageing father, who was so pleased to have his son living close by. Theo was losing more than his job. He was losing his home, his family, his lifestyle. All because of her.

Which was why, ultimately, it was up to her and her alone to set matters right.

Stepping close, he slipped his arms around

her. 'I'm surprised you're letting this get to you, Annie.'

She shrugged. 'It's been a big week. A bit of a roller coaster, actually.'

'It has indeed.' He began to massage her shoulders. 'You need to relax.' Nuzzling her neck, he murmured, 'Why don't you put yourself in my tender care? I suggest an early night. Problems always look much better in the morning.'

Not this time, Theo.

Oh, God. The very thought of the action she must take in the morning made her tremble with terror. How could she do it?

She mustn't think of it now, or she would break down in front of him. She had to focus on what was left to her. This night.

'Your tender care is exactly what I need,' she told him and she turned and slipped into his welcoming embrace.

CHAPTER TEN

ANNIE had known it was going to be hard, but not this hard.

Three times she'd tried to dial Claudia's number and three times she'd chickened out. How could she ever bring herself to do what she knew she must?

Dripping with dread, she stood in the middle of the kitchen and forced herself to stare at the phone. *It will only get worse if I keep putting it off. I've got to do it this time.*

There was no other way. She'd lain awake for most of the night thinking and agonising and she knew this was the only solution.

It broke her heart to realise that she'd caused Theo so much trouble by falling in love with him. At first she told herself it was okay because she hadn't known, hadn't dreamed that she could be creating problems for him.

But she'd read in one of his books about Chinese philosophy that even when you're not wholly responsible for a situation, you have an obligation to find the best way through it.

Which meant she had to accept the awful reality that her presence here was a problem for Theo. She was a threat to his career, and to his happiness as well. And it was up to her to do something about it.

It wasn't fair. It wasn't fair at all that a jealous, vindictive woman like Claudia could cause so much unhappiness, but Annie knew she had to be the one to make amends.

Last night she'd lain beside Theo while he slept and she'd held his hand against her heart and covered him with soft, secret kisses and worshipped him in silence. And then this morning he'd woken refreshed and ready to go to the university to begin grading examination papers and she'd had to find the courage to say goodbye to him, knowing—heaven help her— that it was for the last time.

It had nearly killed her to stand at the back door and watch him walk out of the house with no idea that he'd never see her again. When he turned back and waved to her she'd almost weakened and run to him.

But somehow she'd managed to let him go.

All that was left to do now was this...

Just remember you're doing it for Theo. Think of him, not yourself.

A scared little cry broke from her lips as she dashed across the kitchen and snatched up the phone. *Think of Theo.* She'd already found the direct number for Claudia's office in a note-book beside Theo's phone and her hand shook as she punched the digits.

Oh, please let the connection go through. I couldn't bear it if I have to spend ages waiting, or if I'm asked to call back later.

'Claudia Stanhope speaking.'

Gulp. *Oh, help.* 'Claudia, good morning. This is Annie—Annie McKinnon.'

'Good morning, Annie.' Claudia's response was cool, but she didn't quite manage to hide her surprise. 'How can I help you?'

'I think you'll be able to work that out for yourself.'

'I beg your pardon?'

'I'm ringing to let you know that I'm leav-ing Brisbane and I'm leaving Theo. I'm getting out of his life—going home to Southern Cross.' The words spilled out in a rush, an emotional landslide.

For too long there was silence on the other end of the phone. Then… 'Poor Theo.' And a little later, 'Why are you telling me this, Annie?'

Annie suppressed an urge to scream. 'You know very well why.'

'I do?'

'I'm not going to put myself through the humiliation of spelling it out, Claudia. You've umpteen degrees, so I'm going to trust you to be clever enough to fill in the blanks. Just remember—' Her courage almost failed and she was shaking so badly the trembling vibrated in her voice. 'I'm going to be out of Theo's life. Gone. For *good!*' The last word exploded on a sob.

Oh, Theo.

Slamming the receiver down, she slumped on to a stool.

She'd done it.

She'd done the unbearable. Now all she had to do was get out of here and she would have atoned for the damage she'd caused. Within a day or so, Theo would have his job back and he wouldn't have to leave this house, or his life here in Brisbane.

Oh, God. She'd given him up.

As the full force of her heartbreak crashed over her, she caved forward on to the kitchen bench, unable to control her horrible, noisy, desolate sobbing.

How could she bear this? Theo was the most wonderful man she'd ever met—was ever likely to meet. She loved everything about him—his beautiful smile, his quiet dignity, his mind, his body, his kisses, his touch—his *passion.*

Oh, dear heaven. She had to get a grip. If she thought about the way Theo made love to her, she would be crying for the next hundred years.

A scratching sound on the glass door caught her attention and she turned to see Basil on his hind legs, trying to get inside the kitchen, no doubt worried because he could see how upset she was. Hurrying over to him, she slid the door open, then dropped to her haunches to hug him.

'Oh, you darling boy, I'm going to miss you too.' Still sobbing, she let him lick her tears. 'Look after Theo for me, won't you, mate?'

She hugged Basil hard, rubbing her cheek into his soft coat. When at last she released him, something tugged at her hair and she realised that the old piece of ribbon that she'd used to tie back her hair had caught in his collar. She stared at the narrow strip of yellow silk and then, on impulse, threaded it through the metal ring on Basil's collar and twisted it several times before knotting it.

'This is a friendship band for you, Basil,' she said.

It was a hopelessly teenage-angst sort of gesture, but it made her feel a little better to leave something behind. And it looked kind of cute—that little band of gold against Basil's dramatic black and white coat.

Then, before the tears could start again, Annie jumped to her feet. It was time to call a taxi.

'Is Annie here?'

The question burst from Theo the instant Mel opened her front door and he could hardly believe he'd asked it so calmly. Inside he was *roaring*.

Mel gaped at him. 'Dr Grainger, what a surprise.'

'I'm looking for Annie. Is she here?'

'Here?' Mel repeated, frowning, and the blank look on her face sent Theo's hopes plummeting. 'I thought she was at your place,' she said.

He muttered a curse beneath his breath.

'What's happened?' Mel stepped forward on to the porch and let the door close behind her.

He tried not to feel put off by her lack of welcome. 'Annie's gone and I have to find her.'

'You mean she's packed her bags and left you?'

Left you. The finality of those words echoed and clanged in the cold, hollow emptiness inside him. 'Yes,' he admitted, although it killed him to do so. 'She left a note, but it doesn't make sense.'

Mel's fine eyebrows lowered over worried eyes as she held out her hand. 'May I see the note?'

Theo hesitated. He hadn't intended to hand over something so personal.

'Do you want my help?' asked Mel.

With reluctance he accepted that he had little choice. Mel was an important connection and, the truth of it was, he was desperate. Taking the creased paper from his shirt pocket, he handed over the message he knew by heart.

Dear Theo,
I have to go, and you mustn't try to stop me. Soon you'll understand why and then everything will be fine for you.
    All my love,
    Annie

After scanning it quickly Mel looked up and fixed him with an even grimmer glare as she folded her arms across her chest. Her manner was so fierce that he felt like a very naughty schoolboy being carpeted by the headmistress.

'What have you done to upset her?' she demanded.

'Nothing that I know of.' He sighed. 'I don't think this is about something I've done.'

'Then what's happened?' Mel's eyes shimmered with fury.

'I think it must be a—a situation that's arisen.'

'A situation?' she snapped like a bossy little guard dog.

'It's kind of complicated.'

'Oh, God. Not another woman?'

'Yes.' One glance at her horrified face and Theo rushed to redress his mistake. 'I mean no. I'm not seeing another woman or anything like that, but Annie thinks—' He groaned and shoved anguished fingers through his short dark hair. 'It's way too complicated to explain, but Annie's decided that she's to blame for something that happened—' He sighed again. 'So I take it she hasn't tried to contact you?'

'I'm afraid not. Do you know what time she left?'

'I think it was some time this morning. If she's not here, she might have headed back to Southern Cross.'

'Probably.' She scowled at him again. 'I knew this was going to turn out badly.'

Theo wanted to protest but decided it was wiser not to begin an argument with Annie's friend. 'If you hear from her will you please let me know straight away?'

Her gaze narrowed. Cocking her head to one side, she leant one hip against the porch railing. 'That depends on what Annie has to say, Dr Grainger. She may not wish to have anything more to do with you.'

'Please,' he begged, not caring how desperate he sounded. 'I've got to find her and speak to her.'

Mel didn't answer immediately and if Theo hadn't been so distressed he might have admired her caution.

'You're obviously a very good friend of Annie's,' he said. 'I can see that you're as worried about her as I am but, I promise you, I have her best interests at heart.'

'You do know she's hopelessly in love with you, don't you?' Mel said carefully.

His heart rocked. 'That's why I have to find her.'

There was another agonising stretch of silence, but at last Mel's expression softened. 'Okay,' she said. 'If Annie rings, I'll try to persuade her to contact you.'

'The minute you hear from her?'

She smiled gently. 'Yes, Theo.'

*   *   *

Bouncing on the front seat of the mail truck as it rattled along a dirt track that cut through the heart of the Star Valley, Annie peered through the dusty windscreen, straining to catch her first sight of home. Now that she'd almost completed the long journey from Brisbane via Townsville and Mirrabrook, she wanted this last leg to be over. The closer she got the safer she felt.

She tried to squash memories of the over-excited, bubbly young woman who had raced away from Southern Cross for her date with Damien. She'd known then that she was taking a risk, that things might not work out in the city, but she could never have anticipated that she would be coming home with such a broken and battered pain-filled heart.

Ahead of her a flash of green and white told her that Southern Cross homestead was coming into view and as the truck bumped along the gumtree-lined track, she glimpsed more and more details—the silver flash of the ripple iron roof, the smooth green sweep of lawn in front of the house, the bullnosed overhang on the deep, shady verandas—and then—a black and white streak shooting around the side of the house.

Lavender, her Border collie.

Leaning out of the open side window, Annie

waved to her. 'Poor Lavender's missed me,' she told Ted, the mail truck's driver. But Ted wasn't a talker so a nod and a grin were the most she could expect from him.

It was so weird the way Lavender always knew when she was coming home. Weird, but wonderful. Wonderful to know that, whatever else happened in this crazy world, faithful Lavender's loyalty would never falter. Her dog's love would always be waiting for her.

Oh, help. She forced herself to mentally edit out the other black and white dog she'd fare-welled yesterday.

'Are you going to stop for a cup of tea?' she asked Ted.

He grinned and nodded. 'I could do with a cuppa. Throat's a bit parched.' It was the longest speech he'd made all morning.

As soon as he'd guided the truck to a halt near the homestead's front steps, Annie threw the door open and succumbed to Lavender's enthusiastic greeting. 'Hey, baby, you've got to calm down,' she said with a laugh. 'Yeah, I love you, too, sweetheart. Okay, why not lick me to death?'

When at last Lavender calmed down and Annie stood up, she looked around expec-tantly. Where was everyone? She knew that Reid was still filling in for the manager at

Lacey Downs, but there was no sign of Vic, the gardener, or her brother Kane, or the English housekeeper who'd been filling in while she'd been away.

Somehow she didn't think she could bear to come home to an empty house.

'Hey, Kane, where are you?' she called.

It was quite possible that he was out working on one of the back blocks, but what about the English girl he'd hired? Annie had hoped that she would still be here, even if she only stayed on for another day or so.

It would be rather nice to have some female company. A welcome distraction from all the thoughts that were tearing her apart.

She walked around to the back of the truck and lifted her bag down and then at last she heard Kane's voice. 'Coming, Annie.'

Thank goodness. With something of a shock, she realised how much she wanted to see Kane. There had been many times, particularly in her teenage years, when her big brothers' teasing had been the bane of her existence, but that had changed after their father had died, and right now she couldn't think of anyone she'd rather see.

Then suddenly there was Kane, loping down the front steps—a tall, sandy-haired figure in typical outback working clothes—cotton shirt, blue jeans and dusty riding boots. Annie threw herself into his big, strong embrace and clung to him. And Kane, bless him, hugged her tightly and pressed her head against his massive shoulder and held her as if he understood exactly how she felt.

When he released her, he held her at arm's length and studied her. 'I wasn't expecting you so soon. How are you, sis?' he asked gently.

'I'm—' She drew a deep breath. 'I'm okay.'

He frowned. 'You sure?'

'Yep.'

'You look a little—strained.'

She shrugged and looked away. It was going to be hard to keep a stiff upper lip, but it would be worse to start talking about her heartache. Her pain was still too fresh and raw and she just knew that she'd break down and upset Kane. Next thing *he'd* be on a flight to Brisbane threatening to rip poor Theo to shreds.

But she couldn't just stand here staring at her toes. She looked up at Kane and was suddenly shocked by the scary bleakness in his blue eyes and the uncharacteristic tension in the set of his jaw and his shoulders.

'You don't look so great yourself,' she said. 'Is everything okay?'

Kane seemed distracted and turned abruptly

away from her to the mailman. 'Hey, Ted,' he said. 'Sorry I didn't say good day. Will you be able to take another passenger with you on your way back into town?'

'I reckon I could,' Ted said, nodding.

'Who's that?' Annie asked. 'Not the English girl?'

Kane shot her a sharp glance. 'You know about Charity?'

'Reid told me you had someone here to do the housework.'

He nodded slowly.

'Is she leaving already?'

'Yeah.' He kicked at a clump of grass with the toe of his riding boot.

'That's a pity. I was hoping she could stay on for a bit.'

'She's rather keen to get away.'

Kane's voice was casual enough, but he stared so sadly into the distance that Annie was suddenly certain her brother was hiding something—something that could only have happened while she'd been gone.

Given her own misery as well as Kane's, it was becoming horribly clear that she should never have left Southern Cross for the city.

When Reid McKinnon came back from his stint at Lacey Downs it took him no time at all to work out that something was very much amiss with both his siblings.

'What's been going on while I was away?' he demanded at dinner on the first evening. 'Have you two been sick or something? Annie looks as if she hasn't slept for a month. And Kane, you look like you've been sentenced to life imprisonment.'

Annie and Kane exchanged self-conscious shrugs. They'd both been sympathetic to each other's misery, but they'd avoided delving too deeply into their problems. Even so, Annie was almost certain that Kane's gloominess was directly related to the departure of the English girl, Charity Denham.

Charity was incredibly pretty, with lovely auburn hair, clear green eyes and gorgeous skin, and when she'd said goodbye to Kane it had been impossible to miss the chemistry between them. Why had Kane let her go?

Crikey! What a pair she and Kane were— both lovelorn losers.

When neither of them replied, Reid gave up and resumed eating, but Annie knew he wouldn't let the matter drop, even though he diplomatically changed the subject and gave them a report on the condition of the stock at Lacey Downs instead. She knew that Reid was doing his Big Brother act—watching them carefully and waiting for the right moment to question them separately.

As it turned out, he confronted Annie mid-morning the following day.

'Wow! They look snazzy,' he said, coming into the washroom when she was in the middle of ironing her pink jeans.

'Thanks,' she said cautiously.

He lounged a denim-clad hip against the door frame and she waited for him to follow up with a wisecrack about her new citified taste in fashion.

'I guess you bought them in Brisbane.'

'Yep, under the expert guidance of Mel and Victoria.'

Shifting his weight to lean a bulky shoulder against the doorjamb, Reid watched her in silence for a moment or two. 'So how was the break in Brisbane?'

'Great.'

'Was it long enough?'

Surprised, she stared at him. 'I—I guess so.'

'You came home in a bit of a hurry, didn't you?'

She shrugged.

'And you look like hell, Annie.'

Oh, help. His grey eyes were regarding her

with such obvious concern and he had said this so gently that she almost broke down.

I feel absolutely awful, Reid. There are so many broken pieces inside me, I'm not sure I'll ever heal. And it's getting worse every day.

'Hey, Annie, watch out, you'll burn a hole in those new jeans.'

Quickly setting the iron upright, she turned it off at the wall, then hooked the jeans over a coathanger on a cupboard door, and turned to face him once more. She loved both her brothers, but Reid had always been the one she'd turned to when she had really been in trouble. He wasn't a saint. There were times when he'd teased her mercilessly, but he wasn't as hot-headed as Kane; he was more sensitive and a terrific listener. Now, however, he was bent on firing questions.

'Kane tells me you've been refusing to take phone calls from some guy in Brisbane.'

She felt her face flame. 'I can't talk to him.'

'Why? Who is he?'

How on earth could she explain? Her poor tormented brain seemed to be tied in knots and everything about her trip to Brisbane felt too painful and complicated. If she tried to explain about Theo, everything would unravel too fast and she'd probably make a hash of it. She might not be able to make Reid understand that

Theo was wonderful and kind and not at all to blame for her misery.

'You look terrible, Annie. What's the matter? What's this bloke in the smoke done to you?'

'Nothing,' she said quickly.

'You can at least tell me his name.'

'It doesn't matter, Reid. He's—he's just a guy—who—who wants to keep in touch but—' She hesitated.

'But you want to give him the cold shoulder?'

'Yes,' she said in a small voice.

'He's not a stalker, is he?'

'No.'

'Is he making a nuisance of himself, Annie?'

Horrified, she insisted, 'No, nothing like that.'

'Then why do you look so flattened?'

'I think I overdid things in the city. Too much partying. Don't worry about me, Reid. I'll be okay.'

At first Reid let out an irritated grunt and looked as if he wasn't going to accept her weak explanation, but then he seemed to have second thoughts.

With an excessive lack of haste, he relaxed in the doorway again, crossed his arms over his chest and hooked one riding boot in front of the other. 'Maybe a proper holiday would do you good.'

Surprised, she managed, 'Perhaps.'

'How about a total change of scene?'

It occurred to her then that her brother had probably been leading this conversation in a pre-programmed direction from the start. 'Did you have somewhere in mind?'

He shoved his hands deep in the pockets of his jeans. 'I had a long chat with Kane last night.'

'Did he admit that he's in love with Charity Denham?

Reid smiled slowly. 'I dragged it out of him.'

'Good.' Annie blinked. 'I can't blame him. Charity's very lovely.'

'She's that all right. Kane's eating his heart out over her,' Reid said. 'So I've told him he should get cracking over to England to sort things out.'

She felt a rush of excitement for Kane. 'Good for you, Reid. That's excellent advice and he'll listen to you. If you say it's okay, he'll probably go.'

'And I think you should go with him.'

She gaped at him, then rolled her eyes. 'As

if Kane would want me tagging along while he sorts out his love life.'

'But you could fly with him to the UK and visit Mum in Scotland.'

Goodness! Averting her gaze, so Reid couldn't see her reaction, she noticed a fallen clothes peg on the floor and she quickly bent to pick it up, then dusted a fine layer of red outback dirt from it with her fingers.

'Wouldn't you like to go?' Reid asked.

'Y—yes, of course.' At any other time she would love to go. She'd be there in a shot. She'd missed her mother terribly and longed to see her again.

But—she knew it didn't make a jot of sense—but she didn't think she could bear to travel so far from Theo. Even though she could never be a part of his life, the thought of putting so much distance between them was too painful. Scotland was on the other side of the world. 'That would leave you here on your own,' she said.

'Don't worry about me. I can get another ringer from Starburst station if I need to, and I've got a new cook coming over from Richmond in a day or two.'

'What about the book work? I've been away and I need to catch up.'

'I'm sure I'll manage. Those spreadsheets

you've set up on the computer are great, but if there's a problem with the books, Sarah Rossiter will lend a hand.'

Annie waggled the peg at him. 'You mustn't take Sarah for granted, Reid. Heading a one-teacher school must keep her busy enough without running to your beck and call.'

To her surprise, Reid's face darkened. Icy sparks flashed in his grey eyes and a muscle twitched in his jaw. 'Don't ever accuse me of taking Sarah for granted.'

Jeepers, where had *that* come from? Since when had Reid become so touchy about Sarah? 'I'm sorry.'

'Listen,' he said, quickly recovering his usual composure. 'The mustering's finished and it'll be the wet season soon, so we shouldn't be too busy. Kane needs to go now, and you could do with a diversion. I'll be fine. It's perfect timing.'

Reid had it all worked out.

'Can we afford two overseas plane flights? I'm afraid I went ballistic with my credit card in Brisbane.'

He fired a quick gaze at the jeans she'd just ironed and smiled. 'We can manage.'

Dropping the peg back in the appropriate basket, Annie crossed to the washroom window and stared out at the big expanse of sunny blue sky and the stretch of dry, buff-coloured paddock that ran down to the trees lining the creek.

Common sense told her that it didn't matter where in the world she was in relation to Theo. She couldn't communicate with him or see him, so if she was going to be separated from him in the isolated outback she might as well be on the other side of the globe.

Her terrible task was to try to forget about him. She had to avoid Theo at all costs. If she stayed in Queensland she might weaken.

Perhaps being on the other side of the world was her wisest option.

She took a deep breath and then another before she turned back to Reid. 'Thanks for the offer. I'll definitely give it some thought.'

'Don't take too long to make your mind up. Kane's raring to go.'

Theo dropped his pen and pushed away from his desk. It was so difficult to work, so hard to focus. The end of year examination papers had started flooding in and he had a mountain of marking to wade through, but all he could think of was Annie.

Where was she?

Whenever he tried to ring Southern Cross or her mobile he got an answering machine, but none of his messages were returned. His emails to Annie's address had been blocked as well, so he couldn't reach her that way. And yesterday even her friend Melissa had gone silent on him.

If he could, he would jump on a plane and fly to Townsville, then hire a car and drive himself out to the McKinnons' cattle property in the Star Valley. And if Annie wasn't there he wouldn't leave until he'd found someone who would tell him where she was. But he had all these exam papers waiting to be assessed. Unavoidable deadlines loomed.

He'd never felt so hellish, so frustrated, so anguished.

Until now, he'd taken life's setbacks on the chin. He was a philosopher and he'd trained himself to react to disappointments with a certain sang-froid. But Annie's disappearance had dealt a blow that no amount of reason or logic could heal.

He'd told her once that philosophers avoided discussions about romantic love because the emotions involved disrupted more serious occupations.

Damn right. He was a mess. The famous Theo Grainger equanimity had been shot to pieces.

The downhill run had started from the moment he'd seen Annie McKinnon in the lobby at the Pinnacle Hotel. That night he'd been so distracted by her animated, lively loveliness that he'd almost walked into a marble pillar.

And that had been before he'd got to know her.

Since then he'd been totally distracted and walking into metaphorical pillars every step of the way.

Vivacious, fun-loving, gutsy, inquisitive, sensuous—Annie McKinnon was a weapon of mass distraction. She'd worked her way under his skin and straight into his heart. And now she was gone. And Theo was so undone he couldn't think straight.

If only he'd taken more notice of the way she'd blamed herself for his dismissal. At the time her fears about Claudia had seemed so ludicrous that he couldn't possibly take them seriously. But Annie had been convinced, and now—

At the squeak of a door opening behind him, Theo turned to discover Rex Bradley, a fellow lecturer, poking his head into his office.

'Oh, you are here,' Rex said. 'I knocked but there was no answer.'

'I'm sorry, Rex. I didn't hear you.' He raised a hand and made a quick, beckoning gesture. 'Come on in.'

To his surprise his colleague almost skipped into the room.

'You look chipper.'

'I am. I've just come from Claudia's office and I bring glad tidings.'

'You've been promoted?' Theo hoped he would be able to dredge up the necessary enthusiasm.

'Good heavens, man, credit me with some tact. I haven't come to crow over you with news about myself. No, it's great news for you, Theo. For all of us, actually. Her Highness has just announced there will be enough funding for your course to continue after all.'

'She's what?' Theo felt the blood drain from his face.

'Claudia's changed her mind. She's going to renew your contract.'

'That—that's incredible. Why?'

'Who knows? Our Claudia works in mysterious ways. I can only suppose she's had an attack of sanity and remembered what a fabulous lecturer you are and that she'd made a stupid mistake with the budget. But I don't give a hoot for her reasons. The whys and wherefores aren't half so important as the fact that we're not going to lose you.'

'No one else has been sacked instead of me, have they?'

'No, Theo. Trust you to worry about others at a time like this.' Rex paused. 'Curiously enough, Claudia seems to have found a loophole in the funding cut problem.'

Theo stared at Rex and felt an icy flood sluice through him from head to toe. *Annie had been right.* He hadn't believed it possible, but Claudia's sudden about-face was so implausible there could be no other explanation.

'Why hasn't Claudia come to tell me this herself?' he asked.

Rex cleared his throat. 'She made some excuse about a meeting in Sydney and having to rush away to catch a plane. I suspect she might be feeling a bit sheepish about her sudden turnaround. But I promise you, Theo, it's genuine. She asked me to give you the news.'

He held out a memo and Theo shoved it on to his desk without even glancing at it. He was too appalled by the realisation that Annie had sacrificed herself for him. She'd seen through Claudia's game.

It was all so sickeningly obvious now. Just yesterday Claudia had called by his office to see how he was bearing up, and she'd posed several carefully casual questions about Annie. And, poor, ignorant fool that he was, he'd confessed honestly that Annie had disappeared. And when Claudia had pressed him, he'd admitted that he hadn't really known why.

Now it was patently clear that the damned manipulating woman *had* been jealous of Annie. She'd been playing games with his life, with his personal happiness. And, just as Annie had predicted, within a few days of her disappearance his job had been reinstated.

'You don't look too happy, Theo.'

Rex had to be joking. How on earth could he possibly be happy?

CHAPTER ELEVEN

THE week before Christmas was not the best time for a girl from tropical North Queensland to be visiting Scotland. As Annie walked beside the Lake of Menteith, she tried to imagine this scene in summer when it was bathed in sunshine, bordered by lush, green forests and busy with busloads of tourists and fishermen in boats. Now the shores of this romantic lake in the heart of the Trossachs were white and stark. And *so-o-o-o* cold.

Then again, lonely, cold, windswept shores suited Annie's mood. Out here she could feel as bleak as she liked and no one could bother her with well-meaning questions.

Fat snowflakes fell, settling on her head and shoulders as she stared out to the little island in the middle of the lake.

And thought of Theo.

It happened all the time now. It didn't matter what she looked at, where she visited or whom she talked to…she thought about Theo and longed for him. He commanded centre stage in her thoughts first thing in the morning, at noon, and into the long, lonely nights.

Coming to Scotland hadn't helped at all.

It was wonderful to see her mother, of course. Lovely to meet her mother's friends and to get to know the quaint town of Aberfoyle where her mother and her Aunt Flora lived. But Annie hadn't been able to bring herself to talk to her mother about Theo.

What was the point? How would it help to *talk* about him, when what she craved was to see him, to feel his arms around her, to have him with her, in her life. She needed him here beside her.

She longed to share these new sights with Theo. If only she could slip her arm through his and walk with him over this ground. She longed to talk with him...

They would talk about everything...

She could almost hear their voices above the crunching sounds of her boots treading on icy snowflakes...

They would discuss the fascinating history of Rob Roy and the monks at Inchmahome, an ancient priory that had been built centuries ago on the little island in the middle of this lake. She could take him to see her favourite sights so far—the charm of a cluster of pines beside the wee kirk in Aberfoyle, the breathtaking grandeur of Stirling Castle, or the gorgeous stone bridge over the falls at Killin.

But without Theo, Scotland's attractions seemed insignificant and colourless—as stodgy as porridge and as bleak as the leaden skies looming low over the lake.

It was shameful how weak she was. If he rang again, she was sure she would have to speak to him. She should be disciplining her mind, training herself to forget about him, instead of obsessing about him night and day. But how could she ever forget Theo? She knew he was the one, the man she'd been searching for all her life. Her soul cried out for him.

Except… I've given him up and I must forget him.

Oh, help… Time to drive on to check out Loch Katrine.

As she crossed the icy ground to her parked car, her mobile phone beeped and her heart took off like a duck at the sound of a shotgun. How stupid of her. It wouldn't be Theo.

Digging a thickly gloved hand deep in the pocket of her coat, she extracted the phone, but her woollen gloves were so thick she almost pressed the wrong button as she tried to receive the call.

It was Kane's number.

She let out her breath with a whoosh and willed herself to relax.

'Hi, Kane,' she said, raising her voice above the wind. 'How are you?'

'I'm terrific,' he said and she knew immediately that it was true. She could hear his happiness ringing in his voice. 'Charity and I are getting married.'

'Oh, Kane! Oh, wow! That's fantastic!' She let out an excited little squeal. 'When?'

'In a few weeks' time. Here in Derbyshire. You and Mum and Aunt Flora will all have to come, of course.'

'Of course we'll come. We'll be there with bells on. Oh, Kane, I'm so happy for you. Congratulations. You sound so excited.'

'I'm over the moon, Annie. I can't believe Charity wants me. You've no idea how good this feels.'

'I—I guess not.'

'I'll get back to you soon with details, dates, venues et cetera.'

'Yes, okay.'

'Oh, I forgot to ask. How's Scotland?'

'Lovely. I'm driving around the lochs today. How's Derbyshire?'

'It's amazing—has a cute factor right off the scale. Hollydean, where Charity lives, is the sort of place we only get to see on Christmas cards.'

'Everything over here is so pretty, isn't it? Have you rung Reid?'

'Yes, I wanted to tell him first. If it wasn't for the pair of you urging me over here, I'd probably still be at home moping around Southern Cross like a wounded dog.'

'Our pleasure, mate.'

They said their farewells and Annie dropped the mobile back into her pocket. Kane was ecstatic. And she was so happy for him. She was, she really was.

Just the same, as she continued to the car she almost collapsed beneath the weight of a sudden cloud of despair. She tried not to let Kane's happiness highlight her own misery, but she couldn't help it. She felt so instantly black and hopeless; it was as if she'd stumbled into a bottomless hole with no hope of rescue.

She needed Theo more than ever. Now. This moment. Suddenly she knew she had to make contact. She couldn't face another day, another hour, without speaking to him.

Her heart raced frantically as she pictured herself dredging up the emotional courage to telephone him. It would be night-time in Australia, but not so late that he would be asleep. Yes, she would do it. She could justify her call on the grounds that she needed to make sure he'd been reinstated at the university and that her sacrifice had been worthwhile.

Leaning against the side of the car, she pulled off one glove so that she could punch in the international code followed by Theo's number.

Oh, God, what could she say? *I just need to hear your voice?*

Her chest felt so tight she could hardly breathe. At this rate, when Theo answered she would be too breathless to say anything. But she would feel better once she knew that he was all right.

Closing her eyes, she dragged in a deeper breath as she listened to the phone ringing.

Then it stopped and her heart almost shot clear out of her throat.

'Hi, Theo Grainger speaking.'

She experienced a jolt of pure elation. It was so, so good to hear his lovely voice. 'Hi, Theo.'

'I'm afraid I can't take your call. I'm on an extended vacation. Please leave a message after the beep…'

'Oh, no, *no!*'

Extended vacation? Oh, God, no.

That meant the worst had happened—the

very worst. He didn't have his job back; her sacrifice had been wasted.

And now he'd gone away—disappeared beyond her reach.

She couldn't hold back a horrible, harrowing moan. And she was too blinded by tears to find the disconnect button and too devastated to care that her heartbreak was being recorded.

She'd made a mess of everything. Everything! And coming to the other side of the world, which she'd thought was the best, the wisest, thing to do, had been a stupid, terrible mistake.

Standing on the bottom step at Southern Cross homestead Theo felt at a distinct disadvantage, especially as Annie's brother was glaring down at him from the top step, and more especially because the brother's welcome smile had vanished the moment Theo had mentioned Annie's name.

'You came all the way from Brisbane just to speak to my little sister?'

'That's right.' Theo mounted the steps slowly and felt marginally better when he reached the top and discovered that he was much the same height as the scowling brother. Holding out his hand, he said, 'How do you do? I'm Theo Grainger.'

The brother nodded and, although he shook hands, a wary caution lingered in his cool grey eyes. 'Reid McKinnon,' he said, then his lips snapped tightly shut.

'I was hoping to find Annie. Is she at home?'

'I'm not sure that's any of your business.'

So this encounter would be as tough as Theo had feared. He squared his shoulders. 'Your sister may feel differently.'

'I doubt it. You're the fellow who's been ringing her, aren't you? She's refused to answer your calls.'

'Yes, I'm afraid that's right.'

'Can't you take a hint, mate?'

'Believe me, I do understand your concern.'

Reid's eyes betrayed a brief flicker of surprise before he resorted to scowling again. 'You're dead right I'm concerned about Annie. And if you had anything to do with the state she's in, you should be bloody ashamed of yourself, Grainger.'

'State? What do you mean?' Theo's voice seemed to crack and, in spite of his intention to remain calm and polite, he found himself shouting. 'What state? What are you talking about?'

Reid didn't answer.

Pain filled Theo's throat and he felt as if

he'd swallowed a block of marble. 'Where is Annie? What's happened to her?'

At last Reid looked as if he was about to say something, but then he hesitated again.

Theo groaned and slammed one fisted hand into the palm of the other. 'You must understand how I feel about your sister. Do you really think I would travel over a thousand kilometres just to see her if she wasn't immensely important to me?'

Suddenly, from behind him came an explosion of barking and he whirled around to see Basil straining to get out through the passenger window of his hire truck. A Border collie, her tail wagging madly, was barking just as loudly as she leaped to greet him.

Theo spun back to Reid. 'Is that Lavender?'

'Annie told you about Lavender?'

'Of course she did. It isn't possible to know Annie without knowing all about Lavender, is it?'

'I don't suppose it is,' Reid said, looking slightly stunned. 'Hey, Lavender,' he bawled. 'Cut that out.'

The collie ignored him and the tail wagging and frenzied barking continued.

'What's got into her?' Reid muttered. 'Anyone would think those dogs were long lost friends.'

He hurried down the steps and Theo followed him. By now, Lavender was leaping so high she was almost doing back flips and Basil was trying to squeeze through the too narrow gap of open window.

'Stop that right now,' Theo ordered his dog. 'You'll wreck the hire truck.' When Basil ignored him, he strode around to the driver's door and swung it open. Next minute Basil whipped past him.

'Well, I'll be...' said Reid as the dogs found each other. Almost immediately the barking diminished. Lavender began to sniff excitedly at the piece of yellow ribbon on Basil's collar and Theo realised what had caused the fuss.

'That's Annie's hair ribbon,' he explained.

Reid's face flushed and for a moment he looked confused. But then, as he watched the dogs continue to check each other out, his mouth twitched into a puzzled half-smile.

He dropped his gaze to the toes of his riding boots, gave this some thought for a moment or two, then looked up to Theo and assessed him coolly, but his smile was warm as he said, 'Perhaps you'd better come inside. Then you can explain exactly why you're here.'

Jessie McKinnon pushed a plate towards her daughter. 'Have another scone, Annie.'

'I couldn't possibly.'

Sighing, Jessie set her cup and saucer aside and leaned forward. 'You're not well, are you, dear?'

'Of course I am, Mum. I'm fine.'

To Annie's dismay, silver tears glinted in Jessie's eyes. 'I haven't been much of a mother in the past few years,' she said unexpectedly. 'I feel as if I've let my children down.'

'No, Mum.' Despite the loneliness she'd felt over the past six years, Annie knew this wasn't a moment for brutal honesty. Besides, during her time in Aberfoyle, she'd begun to suspect that there were stronger reasons for her mother's absence than she or her brothers had ever guessed.

'We've been fine at home,' Annie said. 'The boys have been fantastic. Anyhow, we bullied you into coming back to Scotland after Dad died and you've simply been a very obedient parent.'

Jessie looked down at her hands in her lap. 'Just the same, my dear, if I'd been a better mother to you, you might have been able to talk to me and tell me what's troubling you.'

Annie's teacup rattled as she set it back on the saucer.

'I've been watching you for weeks now and

you're getting paler and thinner. Flora's noticed it, too. You can't pretend that you're not terribly upset about something, Annie.'

'No,' Annie said softly.

'Is it a man, darling?'

Closing her eyes against the sudden rush of hot tears, Annie nodded.

'You love him?'

Again Annie nodded.

'But he doesn't love you?'

Her eyes flashed open. 'Oh, no, Mum. It's not like that.' Seconds stretched into eternity as their gazes linked and held. Dusky shadows were creeping into the kitchen and in the fading light Jessie McKinnon's lovely blue eyes seemed to shimmer with a dark, secret wisdom as if to say, *You can trust me, Annie. I've had my share of pain and I understand...*

Perhaps it was the compassion in her mother's eyes, or perhaps it was simply the right time, but suddenly Annie knew that she couldn't hold back any longer. She had to tell her mother about Theo before she collapsed from the strain.

It was almost dark by the time she finished her story.

Jessie listened quietly with very few interruptions. Then she rose and hurried to Annie,

giving her a long, hard hug and Annie clung
to her, treasuring the comforting warmth of
motherly arms so long denied to her.

'You poor darling,' Jessie said. 'My poor,
brave girl.'

She didn't offer further comment at first,
and Annie felt suddenly nervous as Jessie
moved quietly about the snug kitchen, turning
on the lights, checking the casserole in the
oven and drawing the pretty floral curtains to
block out the encroaching night.

'How about a pre-dinner sherry while we
talk about this?' she said.

'Thanks.' Annie's nerves tightened a notch.
There was something about the tone of her
mother's voice that suggested she would need
this drink.

As soon as Jessie was seated again and they
each had a glass of sherry in front of them,
Annie said, 'You do think I did the right thing,
don't you, Mum? Don't you agree that I had
no choice but to leave Theo?'

She held her breath as she waited for her
mother's quick reassurance.

But the answer didn't come immediately.
Jessie stared at her sherry glass, twisting its
stem to make it turn slowly.

'Mum?'

Lifting her gaze from the glass to her daughter, Jessie reached out and clasped Annie's hand. 'You've been very brave, Annie. And I'm proud of you.' She paused and seemed to be carefully thinking through what she would say next. 'In every situation there is a better and a worse way to behave, and you saw what you thought was the only right thing to do and found the courage to do what you felt you must.'

'But?' whispered Annie. 'There's a but, isn't there? I can hear it in your voice.' Her insides flinched. Was she strong enough for this? She'd thought she would feel better if she told her mother about Theo. 'What is it, Mum? Tell me quickly.'

Jessie sighed softly. 'I—I can't help thinking that you made one serious mistake.'

'What's that?'

'You didn't consult Theo.'

'But I couldn't!'

'I know that was how you felt, dear, but try just for a moment to think about the situation from his point of view.'

'Of course I've been thinking about it from his point of view. All I ever did was think about what I had cost him. It was because of me that he lost his job. And he was probably losing his house, his life in Brisbane. Everything.'

'So you made a rash decision by yourself and then you left without allowing him any chance to discuss it.'

'But he would have tried to persuade me to stay.'

'Didn't you want to stay?'

Annie moaned. 'Yes, of course I did.' She dropped her head into her hands, then jerked upright again. 'I can't believe you're so down on me.'

'Annie, I'm not down on you. But I know how impetuous you are, darling. Sometimes—' She sighed and left that sentence unfinished. 'What bothers me is that you weren't totally honest with Theo. You didn't tell him everything that Claudia said to you.'

'Because I was sure he wouldn't believe me. I wouldn't have believed it, if I hadn't heard it with my own ears. Claudia's quite beautiful and she's the Top Gun of the philosophy department. Why would a woman in that position be jealous of a clueless little ditzy chick from the bush?'

'I think you're underselling your assets, Annie.' Jessie sighed. 'Okay, even if we leave that aside, you didn't give Theo a chance to come up with his own solution to the problem.'

'That—that's true.'

'Surely it was up to him to decide what was best for his career.'

Oh, God. Annie stared at her mother. She felt winded. Winded *and* wounded. She didn't want to hear this. Struggling to her feet, she began to pace the room. Was her mother right? Had she been totally, totally foolish? A martyr without a just cause?

She'd thought she'd offered Theo a gift of freedom, but had she denied him the chance to make a choice? Theo was mature and patient—a philosopher, trained to think through crises till he reached a reasonable outcome. She, on the other hand, had always been impetuous and rash, swept away by emotions, eager to make the grand gesture.

'What have I done?' she whispered. 'Oh, God, Mum, I've lost him and it's all my own fault.'

CHAPTER TWELVE

IN THE heart of midwinter in the middle of Derbyshire Theo stood in the foyer of the Hollydean Arms and listened to the sounds of dance music and laughter coming from the other side of a set of double doors. Kane McKinnon's wedding reception was in full swing.

And Annie was in there among the wedding guests.

He looked at his watch and wondered when the celebrations would finish. Desperate as he was to see Annie, he had no intention of gate-crashing another man's wedding. He'd convinced himself that it was okay to be here, hovering about outside a function he hadn't been invited to, but he felt uneasy, like an infatuated fan hoping to catch a glimpse of the star he idolised.

Nevertheless, he was prepared to wait here in the foyer and reflect on a sad truth he'd experienced firsthand during the past weeks—a harrowing lesson of the human heart—that the source of a man's greatest joy could become the source of his greatest torment and pain.

He swallowed to rid himself of the knot of tension in his throat. This meeting with Annie would be the most vitally important in his life. He would wait all night if necessary.

Without warning, one of the doors of the reception area opened and a tall, broad-shouldered fellow came into the foyer, tugging at his bow-tie.

He saw Theo and grinned. 'I can't wait to get out of this clobber.'

The clues fell into place in an instant—the man's Australian accent, his blue eyes so like Annie's, his formal suit and bridegroom's buttonhole.

Theo hurried forward, offering an outstretched hand. 'You must be Kane McKinnon.'

'Yeah, that's right.'

'Congratulations.'

'Thanks.' As the bridegroom shook hands, his silver-blue gaze narrowed and gave Theo the once-over. 'Have we met?'

'No. I'm Theo Grainger. Your brother, Reid, directed me here.'

'Grainger...ah, yes.' Kane's face broke into a grin. 'Now I know who you are.'

'Reid mentioned me?'

'When he rang yesterday to wish me luck for the wedding, he told me all about you, Theo.' Kane thumped his shoulder. 'I must say you made a pretty good impression on my brother.'

'I think we hit it off—quite well.'

'Two of you got on like a bushfire, from what I hear.' Kane cocked his head to one side and his eyes turned shrewd. 'Sounds like you've made a big impact on my sister, too.'

Bingo. The raw knot in Theo's throat tightened. Again he tried to swallow. 'That—that's why I'm here. I need to speak to Annie.'

Kane chuckled and he gave Theo's shoulder another friendly thump. 'Looks like the airlines are doing a roaring trade with lovelorn Aussie blokes. I know exactly what you're going through, mate. You feel like hell, don't you? Listen, I'm supposed to be getting changed. Charity and I are heading off soon, but I'll just duck inside and find Annie for you.'

'There's no need to disturb her. She's probably enjoying herself. I—I can wait a little longer.'

Kane favoured him with a who-are-you-trying-to-kid smile. 'Don't talk rubbish, man. Of course you can't wait.'

*   *   *

How much longer could she last? All around Annie, wedding guests were smiling, chatting, laughing and drinking and her face was aching with the effort of holding her smile in place.

It hadn't been so bad at the church. The groom's sister was more or less expected to sniffle and weep during the beautiful and moving wedding ceremony, but it would be rather bad form if she sobbed her way through the reception as well.

Not that she wasn't happy for Kane and Charity. They were both so obviously in love it was impossible not to be thrilled for them. And the reception had been very enjoyable so far—even when she'd been dragged around the dance floor by the local headmaster, the bank manager and by Charity's young brother, Tim.

Problem was, a wedding celebration and a badly broken heart were not a comfortable combination. And it was so hard to avoid thinking about what might have been—if she hadn't been such an impulsive fool. Instead she was left with the consequences of her recklessness—this ghastly cold, unbearable emptiness inside her.

'Annie.'

There was a tap on her shoulder and she turned to find Kane grinning down at her.

'Hey,' she said. 'Aren't you supposed to be getting changed?'

'Yeah. I just ducked back because I've got a message for you.'

'Oh? What is it?'

'There's someone outside who wants to speak to you.'

'Really? Where?'

'Waiting in the foyer.'

She frowned. 'But no one here knows me. Are you sure I'm the one wanted?'

His grin grew wider. 'Absolutely.' Reaching down, he grabbed her elbow. 'Come on. Get a wriggle on.'

'All right.' Puzzled, she stood and smoothed the softly flaring skirt of her fine woollen dress. Across the table she caught her mother's eye. 'I'm just popping outside for a moment.'

Jessie smiled, gave her a brief wave, and continued chatting to the bride's uncle, who was sitting beside her.

'Go through those doors over there,' Kane said, pointing and giving her a gentle shove.

'Who am I looking for?'

'You'll see.' Then he muttered that he had to go, and he took off quickly, heading for a different exit.

How weird.

Making her way through the throng of

happy wedding guests, Annie tried to think who could possibly want her. Her mother and Aunt Flora were both here in this room. Charity was upstairs, getting changed out of her bridal gown, and she didn't need Annie because she had a swag of girlfriends to help her. Annie didn't really know anyone else in Hollydean.

There was always Charity's brother, Tim, of course. He'd worked at Southern Cross as a jackaroo. It could be him. Perhaps he was planning to tamper with the honeymooners' car—tin cans on the bumper bar—Just Married written in shaving cream—confetti in their suitcases. But surely the bridegroom wouldn't have fetched her for that task?

Pushing the nearest of the double-doors open, she stepped out into the hotel's reception area.

And her heart almost stopped.

The foyer was practically empty, but over by the stand of tourist brochures there was a man who looked so much like...

It *was*...

Theo.

It really was him.

She couldn't move. Her heart seemed to lie still in her chest and her body was frozen to the spot by a sudden deluge of emotion. But her eyes were drinking him in.

Theo.

Theo, looking absolutely gorgeous—tall and cuddly in a thick cream cable-knit sweater and brown corduroy trousers. Theo, looking drop-dead sexy in his dark-rimmed glasses. Theo, looking unbelievably worried, his face drawn and his eyes almost haunted. Oh, the poor darling.

It felt like an age but must have been seconds before her sense of paralysis faded. Her heartbeats returned and kicked up to a frantic pace. She was trembling all over, but she took a shaky step towards him and then another.

'Hello, Annie,' he said in a strangely rough, tight voice.

'Hi, Theo.'

She stared at him, hardly daring to believe that this was really happening. She couldn't be dreaming, could she?

'I—I was passing through.'

Passing through? What did that mean? Was he here for five minutes? Five days? She felt terribly confused. There seemed to be a thousand questions she needed to ask, but she couldn't deal with them. Not now. Not when a miracle had occurred and Theo was *here*.

'I'm so pleased to see you,' she said.

'Are you?' He still looked impossibly worried.

'Oh, yes, Theo. I've almost died from missing you.'

And Theo, darling man that he was, held out his arms to her. And suddenly she was rushing, hurtling forward, falling into his embrace.

'Oh, Theo, I can't believe it's you.'

He was real. She clung to him and he hugged her tight against his bulky sweater. Oh, how good it was to touch him, to know for sure that she wasn't dreaming.

He felt huge and wonderful. His body was deliciously strong and hard beneath the layer of soft wool and, as his arms held her close, she could hear his heart beating as fast and hard as her own. Oh, he felt so, so good.

She touched his cheek.

He touched her hair.

Ignoring the group of curious hotel guests walking past, they leaned apart to gaze into each other's eyes with wondrous, disbelieving delight and then they embraced again, holding each other tightly, fiercely, both too overcome, too thankful, too happy for words.

But at last Annie felt compelled to confess. 'I tried to ring you in Brisbane, but I only got your answering machine and I didn't know how else to find you. I've done everything wrong. I'm so sorry.' She looked up into his dear, familiar face. 'I've been terrified that I might never see you again.'

His smile wobbled and his throat worked as if he were dealing with emotions as strong as her own. It was too much for Annie. Her vision turned watery and her eyes filled with tears and she had to press her face into his chest and will herself not to spoil this miracle by sobbing all over him. But she did cry and he seemed to understand and for quite some time he stood there, not saying anything, simply holding her and gently stroking her hair.

At last she was calmer and she lifted her face, swiping at it with one freed hand while she clung to him with the other. She tried to smile. 'You've no idea how good it is to see you.'

He managed a beautiful smile. 'I think you may have mentioned it. I've missed you, too, you know.'

'Theo, I'm so sorry. I'm sorry I left the way I did. I thought I was doing the right thing.'

'I know. I know.'

'I made a mess of everything.'

'*Claudia* made a mess of everything.'

'But I shouldn't have run away and I was so silly. I wouldn't answer your calls and I blocked your emails.'

He toyed gently with a straying curl near her ear. 'You've been a thorough nuisance, Annie.'

'Will you ever forgive me?'

'What do you think?'

She could read the answer in his eyes and she almost expected that he would kiss her.

But instead he touched the V neckline of her heather blue wool dress. 'This is very elegant.'

She shrugged and smiled. 'I thought naked shimmer might be a bit much for the good folk of Hollydean.'

'They don't know what they're missing.'

His smile was of the very private, bone-melting kind, and she wanted so badly to kiss him, but then she remembered exactly where they were.

'How on earth did you know about Kane's wedding? How did you know where to find me?'

He smiled slowly. 'I'm lucky to have your brothers on side. Reid sent me here.'

'Dear old Reid. He's done good turns for both Kane and me now. But you didn't come all this way just to—to see me, did you?'

'Why shouldn't I?'

'You've got so many problems to sort out. Your phone message said you were on extended leave. That's a polite way of saying you've been sacked, isn't it? I was so devastated when I realised that I didn't even save your job.'

'But you did, Annie.'

She blinked at him. 'What do you mean?'

'It happened exactly the way you predicted. As soon as Claudia knew that you were gone, my contract was miraculously up for renewal again.'

'Really?' Already she could feel a layer of guilt peeling away. 'That's wonderful.'

'But I told Claudia she could stick her job some place that's highly uncomfortable.'

Annie gasped. 'Crumbs, Theo, I wish I'd been there. I can't imagine you telling anyone to do that. You're always such a perfect gentleman.'

'You know very well that I'm not.' His eyes flashed with a sudden unmistakable hunger that sent a thrill shimmying straight to her centre. With reverent fingers he traced the curve of her cheek. 'Annie, you don't get it, do you? You're more important to me than any job. There's no way I would consider working for Claudia after what she did to us.'

She wanted to laugh and cry at once. Was it possible to feel this happy without bursting? 'Theo, you mustn't say such lovely things to me in a public place. I'm likely to show my gratitude in an unseemly manner.'

'That's my responsibility,' he said and, without a care for the people in the foyer, he pulled her in to him and kissed her and he took a scrumptiously long time about it.

'You've no idea how much I missed you,' he murmured against her lips.

'Show me again,' she murmured back, winding her arms around his neck.

And he kissed her some more and Annie could feel all the hurt and broken pieces inside her becoming whole again.

'Oh, good, you two found each other.'

They were reluctant to separate, but turned to find Kane coming down the stairs, changed into travelling clothes. His grin was wide. 'Looks like it's a happy reunion.'

Theo and Annie shared rapturous smiles.

Kane crossed over to them and dropped a kiss on her cheek and slapped Theo's shoulder. 'The name Theo Grainger rings a bell,' he said.

'Theo's a philosopher,' Annie told him proudly.

'A philosopher? Oh, must be a different guy then. The one I was thinking of played Rugby Union for Queensland.'

Theo looked surprised. 'I played a couple of seasons for the state team. Years ago.'

Kane nodded. 'Thought it must be you. You were a brilliant winger.' He winked at Annie. 'You did well to catch this guy. He can run like the wind.' He glanced towards the hotel entrance. 'It's a pity I can't hang around and be sociable, but my wife will be down soon and she's expecting a honeymoon.'

'You bet I am.'

Charity, with her lovely auburn hair bouncing about her shoulders and dressed in an elegantly long black coat and boots with a multicoloured scarf at her throat, came hurrying down the stairs. Following her came her bridesmaid, carrying the bridal bouquet.

Annie made hasty introductions.

'Nice to meet you, Theo.' Charity tucked her arm through her husband's and smiled at them. 'I suppose I should join Kane in saying it's a pity we're leaving so quickly, but you wouldn't believe me, would you?'

'No way.'

'We've kept it a secret, but we're off to Paris,' Charity whispered, her eyes shining with excitement and happiness.

'How fantastic.' Annie kissed them both. 'Have an absolute ball.'

Word soon spread that Charity and Kane

were downstairs and ready to leave and soon the wedding guests were crowding through the doors into the foyer, all keen to farewell them. Among them was Jessie McKinnon and when she saw that her daughter was holding hands with a tall, dark and handsome man, her eyes widened with delighted interest.

'Theo?' she mouthed to Annie across the foyer.

Annie nodded and they exchanged excited grins and Annie tingled with happy pride.

Then the guests were all crowding around Kane and Charity as they headed for their car, which was parked in the street outside.

'The bride's about to toss the bouquet,' Theo said. 'Do you want to stay to catch it?'

'I didn't think philosophers would hold with such superstitions.'

He smiled. 'You're right. Besides, you don't need to catch a bouquet. As your brother said, you've already caught me.'

Her heart clattered. Good heavens, was she terribly focused on weddings at the moment, or did that almost sound like a proposal? Electrified, Annie glanced quickly around her at the crowd of people. Everyone's attention was focused on the bridal couple in the doorway.

Theo's attention however, was concentrated

directly on her. And now she couldn't drag her eyes from him—even when an excited babble broke out behind them, which she presumed was Charity's girlfriends trying to catch the bouquet.

Theo took her hand. 'Do you think anyone would mind if we slipped away somewhere?'

'No, it's what my mother has been suggesting with her not very subtle handwaving gestures.'

'She has?'

'Absolutely.'

Hungry for privacy, they almost ran out of view through the doorway into the now empty dining room. Surrounded by the flowers, candlelight and streamers that had decorated the wedding reception, Theo swept Annie close.

'I love you, Annie.'

'Oh, Theo, I love *you*.'

Hearts hammering in unison, they kissed impatiently, hungrily, deeply, their bodies pressing closer, desperate for intimate contact.

When at last he released her, Theo took Annie's hands in his. 'You're coming with me to Rome.'

'To *where*?' she whispered, breathless with shock.

He smiled and dropped a quick kiss on her nose. 'To Rome—in Italy—that country you claim to love—the one where everyone speaks Italian.'

'But—but—'

'I'm on my way there now. I've scored a Research Fellowship and I'll be working at the University of Rome for the next six months.'

'Oh, Theo, how fantastic for you.'

'Fantastic for us, Annie. I'm not going to let you out of my sight again. Besides, I promised I'd take you to Rome and now it's going to happen.'

She stared at him, too stunned to speak.

Watching her, Theo frowned and he looked so endearingly anxious she couldn't resist a playful smile. 'But I've—um—made a New Year's resolution to be less impulsive.'

He released a soft little sound, half-sigh, half-chuckle. 'Trust you to become sensible just when I need you to be reckless.' With a hand beneath her chin, he tipped it up so that her mouth was angled just so and he kissed her again, more slowly this time. Against her lips, he murmured, 'You can learn the language and then we can seduce each other in sexy Italian.'

'Goodness,' she said in a breathless voice, 'you sure know how to make things difficult for a girl who's decided to become less impulsive.'

'Don't worry, Annie, I've done enough deep and serious thinking for both of us. I've even squared this plan away with your brother, Reid. *And* with your dog.'

'My dog?'

'I've left Basil at Southern Cross. He and Lavender are the best of mates and she's stopped moping, so you won't have to feel bad about abandoning her for six months.'

Annie's mouth gaped open.

Theo smiled and kissed her open lips and then he nuzzled her cheek close to her ear. 'Everything's organised, Annie, so you'd better prepare yourself for the fact that you're coming to Rome with me. If you try to say no, I'm just going to pick you up and carry you off.'

Annie grinned. 'No need, Theo. I'd swim to Italy to be with you.'

They arrived in Rome in the early hours of the next day, after a night that had passed like a dream. First they'd shared their news with Jessie McKinnon and received her enthusiastic blessing, and then they'd packed Annie's things and driven in Theo's hire car from Hollydean to London, slept in snatches on the flight from Heathrow to Fiumicino Airport, and taken in the first sights of Rome as their taxi sped them to their apartment.

Finally they set their bags down.

'You must be exhausted,' said Theo.

'I'm too happy and excited to be tired. I can be tired later.' Annie spun in a circle to take it all in. 'This is just lovely.'

The apartment had a tiny kitchen and a large living room, cool tiled floors, stucco walls and wooden beams. The furniture was simple— old-fashioned couches and a timber table with two chairs by a shuttered window. A bowl on the table held a welcome gift of luscious, ripe pears. And in the next room there was an enormous iron bed covered with a white woven spread.

Taking Annie's hand, Theo led her to the window and pushed open faded blue door-length shutters. 'What do you think of the view?'

In the pearl-grey light of dawn, she stepped out on to a tiny balcony with lace ironwork and pots planted with pink geraniums and wild mint. In the distance she could see the rounded curve of a hill, and the silhouette of trees against the lightening Roman sky. She let her gaze travel over the sea of dark rooftops and the occasional dome or spire.

Closer, illuminated by a streetlight, she saw

a row of apartment buildings, centuries old and painted bitter lemon, tomato and rosy grey. Then she looked below and saw a little cobbled square where tables and chairs were set outside a café, and a fountain trickled water from the mouths of two stone dolphins.

'This is it,' she said in breathless awe, leaning back against Theo as he wrapped his arms around her. 'This is Trastevere, isn't it? And it's exactly the same view that you told me about.'

'Do you like it?'

'Oh, Theo, I *adore* it.' She turned in his arms and kissed him, let her lips trail from his gorgeous mouth to the scrumptious underside of his jaw, to his delectable earlobe.

Theo closed his eyes. 'Annie... Annie, have you any idea what you do to me?'

'Mmm.' With her fingers, she traced the line of his jaw then slipped them inside the open neck of his shirt and played with the lovely straight line of his collarbone, savouring the knowledge that soon, very soon now, she would be able to touch all of him.

His hands bracketed her hips, keeping them hard against his as he kissed her brow, her cheek, her chin, her ear. 'You do know how much I love you, don't you?'

He had already told her this in Hollydean,

at Heathrow, and on the plane…but it was perfectly wonderful to hear it again now that they were so very alone. Together at last in their own fascinating, exciting, private home from home. She nuzzled his neck. 'I love you more, Theo.'

'Uh-uh. I don't think you understand how very important you are to me.'

'Well, I need *you* to understand that I'd go with you anywhere. It's wonderful to be here in Rome, but I would have been deliriously happy with you in a grass hut in the jungle.'

'Will you marry me, Annie?'

Goodness, how much excitement could a girl handle? Was it possible to melt from happiness?

Just the same, Annie found herself hesitating… She looked away. There was just one little problem…

'Sweetheart, you're welcome to be as impulsive as you like.'

She lifted her gaze back to his. 'Theo, I'd marry you anywhere, any time, just as I'd live with you anywhere. The only thing is—'

'*What?*' His voice cracked beneath the terrible weight of that single syllable.

'I told my father before he died that when I got married it would be at Southern Cross. It was a silly promise to make, I realise that now—but it's been a—a girlish dream of mine.'

There was a fleeting flash of disappointment in his eyes, impossible to hide, but he recovered in a moment and the tender smile he gave her was his most beautiful yet. 'I wouldn't want to tread on your dreams, Annie.'

'You really are the most darling, darling man.'

'But we can be engaged,' he insisted. 'In fact, we'll go out and buy an engagement ring today. I want to announce to the world that Annie McKinnon is my woman.'

She had thought she was as happy as it was possible to be, but now as the sun climbed above the distant hill, coating the rooftops of Rome with an apricot glaze, and as she and Theo turned back into their new little home, Annie experienced the deepest happiness of all.

She knew now that whatever the future brought she would share it with this man. A lifetime of loving awaited her.

And this was just the beginning.

passionate powerful provocative love stories

**Silhouette Desire delivers
strong heroes, spirited heroines
and compelling love stories.**

Desire features your favorite authors,
including

Annette Broadrick,
Ann Major,
Anne McAllister
and Cait London.

**Passionate, powerful and provocative
romances *guaranteed!***

For superlative authors, sensual stories
and sexy heroes, choose Silhouette Desire.

passionate powerful provocative love stories

Harlequin Historicals®
Historical Romantic Adventure!

From rugged lawmen and valiant knights to defiant heiresses and spirited frontierswomen, Harlequin Historicals will capture your imagination with their dramatic scope, passion and adventure.

Harlequin Historicals . . . they're too good to miss!

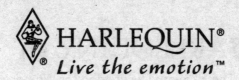

HARLEQUIN®
Live the emotion™

Upbeat,
All-American Romances

 flip**side**

Romantic Comedy

Historical,
Romantic Adventure

INTRIGUE

Romantic Suspense

The essence of
modern romance

Seduction and passion
guaranteed

Emotional,
Exciting, Unexpected

Sassy, Sexy, Seductive!

HDIR204